A Door in the Woods

Book One of the
JIMMY FINCHER SAGA

A Door in the Woods

BY JAMES DASHNER

BONNEVILLE BOOKS
Springville, Utah

ISBN: 1-55517-697-6
e. 2

Published by Bonneville Books
Imprint of Cedar Fort Inc.
www.cedarfort.com

Distributed by:

Cover design by Nicole Williams
Cover design © 2005 by Lyle Mortimer

Printed in the United States of America
10 9 8 7 6 5 4 3 2 1

Printed on acid-free paper

Library of Congress Cataloging-in-Publication Data

Dashner, James, 1972-
  A door in the woods / by James Dashner.
       p. cm. -- (The Jimmy Fincher saga ; bk. 1)
Summary: From Duluth, Georgia, fourteen-year-old Jimmy Fincher sets off
on a quest that takes him across the country and to other, sometimes
terrifying, worlds, armed with a powerful gift and a mission: to prevent
the evil Stompers from destroying Earth.
  ISBN 1-55517-697-6 (pbk. : alk. paper)
[1. Science fiction.] I. Title. II. Series.

PZ7.D2587Do 2003
[Fic]--dc21

                              2003004511

This book is dedicated to my mom.

Everything I have in life, I have because of her.

OTHER BOOKS BY JAMES DASHNER

A Gift of Ice

BOOK TWO OF THE JIMMY FINCHER SAGA

The Tower of Air

BOOK THREE OF THE JIMMY FINCHER SAGA

War of the Black Curtain

BOOK FOUR OF THE JIMMY FINCHER SAGA

✧Acknowledgments✧

There are too many people to thank. I want to thank the people at Cedar Fort for believing in this story, mainly Chad Daybell and Lee Nelson. I also want to thank all those people who took the time to read and reread my manuscript, and weren't afraid to tell me when I'd goofed.

I'm especially thankful to my family. My wife Lynette was a believer from the very beginning, and wouldn't let me give up. I'm also thankful to my kids, just for being my kids, and such good ones, too.

And finally, I want to give a big thanks to Chad Lichliter. Although many people had told me that they liked my book, I didn't truly believe it until Chad convinced me. He was fourteen at the time, and it's for people like him that I created Jimmy Fincher.

✧TABLE OF CONTENTS✧

✧ ✧ ✧

✧PROLOGUE✧

Before I begin the story that will change your life forever, I guess I should introduce myself. My name is Jimmy Fincher and I was born and raised in Georgia. I'm fourteen years old and I love anything to do with sports. I hate cooked peas. And oh, yeah—I absolutely, positively cannot be destroyed.

Well, hearing that last part, if you didn't think I was crazy, then I'd think you were crazy.

I'll be the first to admit what a ridiculous statement it is—it sounds like something from a bad comic book. If someone ever told me that they couldn't be destroyed, I wouldn't think they were crazy because I'd just assume they were kidding. But—whether fortunately or unfortunately, I haven't quite figured out yet—that little statement is as true as saying that cooked peas taste like sewage and smelly feet.

It is very true, and because of it, my life has been taken away from me.

I grew up in a happy home. I probably sound like an adult saying that, but it's the only way to put it because my growing-up years in that home are very over. I have a mom and a dad and an older brother named Rusty. There's no doubt about the happiness of my life growing up in that very humble two-story house in Duluth, Georgia. The whole house was made of wood, and despite the constant pecking of those dang woodpeckers, I couldn't have asked for a better place to be raised. To me, the definition of warmth and safety will always be that home.

My mom's name is Helen, and she was raised on a farm, like all good mothers should be. She has curly, dark hair, and Dad has always said that she was the prettiest girl to ever walk the fields of South Carolina, and I believe him. My dad's name is J.M., which I've always thought a little funny. Of course, to me, he's Dad, but to others he's always been known as two letters of the alphabet. We do things a little differently in the South.

Dad is tall and has straight, black hair—he wasn't raised on a farm, but he used to race cars, and I think that's pretty cool. Like me, Dad was born and raised in the same sweet southern town that the wooden house still stands in today. Duluth is our home, and there ain't a better town in the good ole U.S. of A.

My brother, Rusty—a nickname he got from the color of his hair—is three years older than me, and his idea of fun is coming up with a new way to torture me. From putting my hand in warm water to make me tinkle in the bed—which never works—to threatening to put me in the oven, Rusty's delight has always been the torture of one Jimmy Fincher, a.k.a. his stinky little brother. But we're friends—always have been and always will be. Except maybe when he's had peanut butter and jelly sandwiches. Rusty Fincher, the only human alive who gets the toots from a P.B. and J.

Then, of course, there's me. I'm the skinniest kid to ever walk the streets of Duluth—a trait which I got from my dad, although he's lost more and more of that trait as the years have gone by. I got my body and face from Dad, but I definitely got my hair from Mom. It's brown and curly, and I don't even bother combing it. That's why Mom likes to keep my hair so short. It doesn't really matter in the end, though, because unless you catch me in the shower or asleep, I've got my Braves hat on.

That's my family, and they're the only possession that's ever mattered to me. I'm a young little cuss, but my parents taught me well, and I appreciate what's important in life.

Now.

I wish I could just go on talking about the good things in life. I wish I could take my time and tell you about the summer vacations to Grandma's house in the middle of nowhere on a farm in South Carolina. About the neighborhood swimming pool and how I was always the best buddy of the lifeguard. About school field trips and being in the gifted class, which brought both embarrassment at being a nerd and joy at being able to challenge the little noggin on top of my skin and bones body.

I'd love to tell you about playing basketball in my neighbor's backyard and playing football in the street that ran by my house.

But there isn't time for all that nice stuff.

It's time to tell my story.

Before I begin, there are things to say. You must prepare yourself. The world is not what you think it is, and the nightmares that sometimes wake you in the middle of a storm may be truer than you think. Every novel you've ever read may not be as fictional as you thought. If I have learned anything, it is that nothing is beyond possible or belief. The world as I once knew it has turned upside down, and I've finally realized that the phrase "truth is stranger than fiction" is not just a stupid cliché.

Now, this is not some silly story about Martians or unicorns or elves or vampires or guys named Doctor Potty.

But it is just as strange, and just as mystical, and just as other-worldly, and because it is true, it is far more wondrous. And terrifying.

My story is far from over, but it has a beginning, and it's time to tell it.

All of it is true.
I promise.

✧ ✧ ✧

It started with a tree.

✧CHAPTER 1✧

Ole Betsy

The nightmare started on a really nice day at the beginning of summer vacation.

My mom's azaleas were still flowery, the dogwoods blossoming all white and pretty, and the backyard smelled like heaven with the honeysuckle. Like I said, I know I'm a young guy, but I appreciate a beautiful day. The air was warm, but not too hot, and the humidity hadn't started suffocating us yet. It was, simply, the kind of day in which a fourteen-year-old boy must climb a tree. Birds were chirping, the sun was shining, and I had just had tomato soup and peanut butter toast for lunch.

Life was good.

I set out across the street from my house that fine day, wearing my Braves hat, with nothing in my head but wanting to climb a tree. Ever since I'd had legs and arms—which was from the very beginning mind you—I'd been a climber of things, and I figured it was a good day to climb the beast of all trees in Duluth—Ole Betsy. Only crazy people name trees—I'm guilty. She was a good tree, and she deserved a name, even if it was a cow name. Ole Betsy was back in the woods behind Mrs. Jones' place, and speaking of cows . . . that poor woman. She looked as big as a barn, and not nearly as pretty. We always used to joke that she'd have to stand in the shower one leg at a time.

Anyway, by the time I got to Ole Betsy, I tingled with

excitement. As I hopped up on the first limb, I took a second to sit there and enjoy the surroundings for a minute—the smell of the woods and the sounds of the birds. It seemed a cruel trick of nature to make me so happy right before I would become so miserable.

I started up the tree. As each limb passed, I grew a little more tired and a little more excited to see the top. Little flecks of this and that jumped in my eyes every now and then, making them burn like fire, but nothing could stop me from climbing. I was a man—or kid—on a mission. I twisted my hat around backwards, like a catcher, and eventually, all those limbs and green leaves started showing signs of blue sky, and my heart pumped like gangbusters.

I had almost reached the top of Ole Betsy, about forty feet above the ground, when things kind of went topsy-turvy. Life for this guy was about to take a turn for the worst.

I remember one time when I was about ten, I rode my bike down a steep road close to my house, going a hundred miles an hour, wind flapping in my face and roaring in my ears, trees and houses and people flying by like humming-birds, just as happy as a junebug, when all of a sudden I was lying on the ground, hurting all over, bleeding like a slaugh-tered hog. It turned out someone had thrown a stick at me, and beating the best odds in history, landed it right in my front tire's spokes, flipping me like a bad NASCAR wreck. I went from happy to dazed-silly in a split instant.

That same sort of thing was about to happen to me on that early summer day.

As I reached for the next limb, I heard some rustling in the woods below me, and then the piercing scream of a lady. The horrible sound from her throat filled the woods like a bombing raid siren in an old World War II movie. I looked down, scared to death, trying to be quiet and see what was down there. A man in a dark, old-guy suit dragged a woman through the leaves, fighting her constant struggles. I couldn't make out much through the branches and leaves. All I knew for sure was that below me stood the worst man I had ever seen. There he was, right below me, just dragging and hurting this poor lady for no good reason. I had the sudden fear that maybe he was going to kill her.

I was scared like I had never been scared before. I started crying. I tried to keep to myself, sobbing with fright, but I must've looked like one of those freakies at the Lawrenceville Carnival. I was so suddenly and unexpectedly terrified, my efforts to stay quiet must've been quite a sight.

Things got worse. I did the dumbest thing you can do when you have yourself a murderer under you. I sneezed. I let out a sneeze that would've made that Snow White dwarf retire. I don't know where it came from, but lucky for me, Mr. Killer didn't hear me. But I did get a nasty little something on my finger, which I proceeded to wipe on my pants like any good, upstanding young man would do.

Mr. Killer continued his struggle with the woman. After another few seconds of fighting, the poor lady collapsed like a drunk skunk. I figured then and there that her life had just been cruelly and unjustly extinguished, with all the feeling of putting out a fire after a campout, and that there would be some awfully sad people come evening. I felt an immediate dagger of pain in my heart for that woman's family, imagined the life-changing hurt that her husband and kids would feel. Death had always scared me, and I had just seen it face to face, and my insides filled with sadness.

But then it turned right into something else. Hatred. I hated that nasty man more than I hated the devil himself. I never knew a person could be that evil before then, and it would prove to be the first in a never-ending series of hard lessons in my life. Every part of my scrawny body filled with anger and hatred towards that beast of a man, and I almost fell out of the tree on account of it.

And then, for the first time in the short history of my life, cutting my thoughts short, I saw something that was completely irrational and unexplainable. Nothing in my life had prepared me to see things that were strange or beyond belief. I was a simple kid in a simple town in a simple family. But what I saw then, right after the collapse of the woman, ripped the "simple" out of my understanding of the rules of the world, and changed my life forever.

A sudden crackle filled the air that sounded like a mixture of static electricity and ripping paper. Below me, although it was impossible to see everything perfectly clear, I saw a strange darkness pass over the area where the man stood, like a plane had just flown over us with the noon sun right above it. Except this shadow was much darker, and it didn't pass on by. I had a hard time seeing it, but it looked like there was suddenly an area below me that had forgotten what time it was and had become the middle of the night, with the light of the day around it doing nothing to its darkness. The branches of the tree below me were silhouetted by blackness.

And then, as soon as it had come, it was gone. All was light again, and I could see the man still standing there.

But the woman had disappeared

I stretched and craned my neck and shifted this way and that on the branch holding me at the time, but I couldn't see her anywhere. With the coming and going of the strange darkness, the lady had vanished from sight.

Unless Mr. Killer had just performed the fastest burial in the history of mankind, that lady had just up and disappeared. My fear and sadness and anger turned into bewilderment and shock. I wondered in vain at what I could have possibly just witnessed. I started to shake, and the tears came back without me knowing that they had ever gone away. I felt alone and scared and hopeless, and panic began to swell inside of me. What I had just seen could not possibly be possible.

Then two things happened, and my day-gone-bad got even worse.

The first is that I finally realized who the killer man was. I didn't know him at all personally, but it finally registered in my brain that I had seen this guy many times. He was none other than the mayor of my little town of Duluth, Georgia. The second thing that happened was worse. All of a sudden that devil in a dark suit looked up, straight into my watery eyes.

As mine met with his, I had the strangest thought that this would be a good time to be one of those flying monkeys from *The Wizard of Oz*.

✧CHAPTER 2✧

Nightmare

Due to several deficiencies in my heritage, I'm not a flying monkey, nor am I Superman, so I was in one heck of a bind. Here I had myself in a tree above the latest murderer of Duluth, Georgia, with no where to go but down. And *down* just happened to be the only and quickest route to where Mayor Borbus T. Duck Jr. was standing, looking up at me.

Yeah, no doubt about it, it's an unfortunate name, even for a killer mayor. And to make matters worse, the man is a junior, meaning his parents were cruel enough to pass the name on to him. If they'd had an ounce of decency in their bones, they would have at least given him a respectable first name to offset the joke-waiting-to-happen awfulness of his last name. And despite his murdering ways, this man had a wife, and her name was Bobette. Borbus and Bobette Duck. Unbelievable. Might as well be called Stinky and Butt-Ugly.

Anyway, there I was, skinny little good-for-nothing, looking down on Borbus T. Duck, city-mayor and woman-killer. I was so scared, I thought I was going to heave up tomato soup all over the place. But I didn't. I wet my pants instead. The shame and embarrassment of knowing that a fourteen-year-old was still capable of doing such a thing filled me. But I promised to tell the truth about my strange journey, and there it is.

Mayor Duck began to climb the tree.

Before I knew it, he climbed up those branches like there was no tomorrow. (Which, by the way, is a phrase that I've never understood. If there was no tomorrow, I guess it'd just be the day after tomorrow. Would a man really climb branches differently if he knew that tomorrow would really be the day after tomorrow? Well, I guess it doesn't matter much, and I better quit straying from this story or it'll never get done. The point is I had a killer named Borbus T. Duck climbing a tree to get me. I sure didn't care if tomorrow was really next week or if yesterday was the week before last Monday. I was a mouse stuck in a cat litter.)

After a few moments of climbing, the mayor stopped, panting like he had just finished a marathon, not more than ten feet below me. And then a real mayor of a real town spoke directly to me. His voice was low and grumbly, just like you'd imagine for a fat guy.

"Son, you're in big trouble. Does your mama know where you are?"

"Yes, sir. And I swear I didn't see you kill that woman down there." As soon as I said it I realized how stupid it was. I shook so bad you could've made scrambled eggs on my head. Actually, that didn't make any sense whatsoever, but you get the point. I'm sure as we get along in this storytelling business I'll get better at it.

"Son," the mayor said, "I didn't kill no woman. My . . . friend and I were just wrastlin', that's all. We're done now, and she ran off back home."

I couldn't help but wonder if all old people really think kids are *that* stupid.

"Yes, sir, I know, sir. I'll never say you're a killer. You were just wrestling, that's all," I said, failing to mention the small fact that I had just seen someone disappear.

Borbus T. Duck looked at me for a long time. I had seen him a hundred times before, but never this close. He was so incredibly ugly and fat as a heifer. It pained me just to look at him, especially with sweat all over his pale, fat face. I guess I had no idea what true fear was like until that moment. I knew if the mayor could kill that woman, he could kill a little squirt like myself. Good thing I'd only downed one root beer that day, or I might have had another accident right then and there.

After having stared at me for what seemed like hours, without saying another word, Mayor Duck started climbing again.

Eight branches, six branches, four branches below me. I tried moving farther up the tree, but I'd already come just about as far as I could go. His grunts as he climbed reminded me of the pigs on my Aunt Lorena's farm. Limb by limb, breaking off leaves and twigs, branch by branch, he inched closer by the second, and there was nowhere for me to go but . . .

It was then that I jumped.

✧ ✧ ✧

I had never before done something so crazy in all my life. I was fifty feet in the air, and all of a sudden I decided I was one of those flying monkeys after all. But I guess I just didn't have much of a choice. I figured I'd rather risk breaking a few bones than getting strangled by the mayor of Duluth, Georgia.

I jumped straight out from my limb, in the opposite direction of the side that the evil old mayor was climbing up. I thought I might be able to catch a limb of the neighboring trees on my way down. For about two seconds, I was having a dandy of a time, but it ended quickly. I grabbed at every limb and branch and who knows what else as I fell, but I couldn't hold on to anything. Limbs and twigs and leaves slapped me and poked me and scratched me. Nothing would stop my fall, despite my desperation in trying to grab anything I could.

Then I hit the bottom branch with something my mom says is hard as a rock—my head.

And it hurt. Bad.

It flipped me back the other way and I landed plumb on my back. At that very moment, I thought I was going to die. My head felt like it was in ice-water, and my back felt like Rusty had just gone to new levels in his torture tactics with me. The only thing I saw before blackness came over me was Borbus T. Duck clambering down Ole Betsy, like a fireman going to his fire truck, with his wicked eyes glaring straight at me.

And that's how my nightmare started.

✧CHAPTER 3✧

The Mansion

I hear Mom yelling my name, but I don't listen; I just keep running. I know I have to get back soon, but I just want to swing on the tire one more time. Rusty is yelling at me that I'm going to be in big trouble, but I can't care less. I get me a great running start, feel like I have run a mile, and then I jump up on the tire and take off over the river like a 747. I'm flying, I'm a bird, I'm a dragonfly! Then I hear the snap, and then I feel the absence of anything holding me back, and then I see the broken rope dangle down past me, and then I am falling fast. My heart is in my throat, and the rushing air as I drop roars around me. The only other sound I hear is an evil laughter, like an angel of the devil come to take me away. It is loud and shrill, like a bird that has just been shot. It reminds me of one of those clown toys I saw at the flea market that just didn't sound quite right when you pulled the string and let it go. Then I realize how strange it is that I haven't hit water yet. I'm just falling and falling but the river isn't getting any closer. I look down, and there is no river in sight. It's been replaced by a thick blackness, empty of light. And all I can hear is that horrible laughter, calling me . . . calling me . . . waiting to swallow me whole . . .

I jerked up from my sleep, sweating like a pig in August. My breath was heavy, and my hair stuck to my forehead. At first I couldn't see a thing—it was pitch black—and I couldn't hear a sound coming from anywhere. I lay in a soft bed, with covers over me, and a nice fluffy pillow. I panicked, but I couldn't get myself to move.

Soon, my eyes adjusted a bit, and I could see a window to my right. Barely any light was coming through at all, but I could tell it was a window. I waited longer still.

A little bit later I finally got the nerve to get up and try to find out what the heck was going on. I sure wasn't in my bed at home, and I sure wasn't in Rusty's room. All I could remember was lying under that tree looking at Mayor Duck coming down at me. As if brought on by the thought, I felt the pain in my head and back again. It ached like nothing else, and I had to sit back down before I passed out.

I felt hopeless. I either started crying again or just kept crying from the first time, I couldn't remember. I was scared to death. Where was I? Where was my mom? Did that devil of a mayor drag me to his shack or what? Where could I—

The door to the room opened.

I gave out a little shriek and jumped back onto the other side of the bed. Before I landed, the light switched on.

Standing in the doorway was the biggest man I had ever seen. He must've been seven feet tall and three hundred pounds. His hair was the color of lemon frosting and his skin as dark as a lifeguard in late summer. He wore one of those fancy suits that old people tend to wear—it was a dark charcoal color. He had demon eyes bearing down on me like a wolf's on a rabbit. Needless to say, I didn't think this monster was going to be too friendly.

Then, the Monster spoke.

"You, get up. Time to go see the Sheriff."

I gave a quick sigh of relief. Monster-boy wasn't going to kill me after all! In fact, he was going to take me to the police and everything would be just fine. Well, I might as well tell you right now, that was not the case.

I slowly got up and gave a quick, "yes, sir," and followed him into the hall. I could finally see what kind of place I was in, and it was nothing but a mansion. The walls were wall-papered all nice and fancy, with frilly wooden thing-a-ma-jiggers along the top and bottom. The white carpet could have made a bed for normal folks like my family, real cushy-like. It felt good under my toes. That was how I realized that I didn't have my shoes on. Somebody had done me the favor of taking them off for me.

We walked down the hall a ways, down some curvy wooden stairs—I think they were made out of cherry wood—through a foyer I swear was bigger than the White House itself, and finally into a huge room that I guess was a library of sorts. You talk about your rich folks. I swear I saw this library in one of those boring movies about England that my mom's always watching. I didn't get too much time to see what it looked like because I wasn't in there more than two seconds before all the lights suddenly went out and I was in the pitch dark, alone with the beast of a man that had brought me there—or at least I *thought* we were alone.

I coughed, and it sounded like a sonic boom in all that silence.

"Hello, young Jimmy, my boy," a raspy voice spoke from the darkness. "Don't be alarmed. Now, you've gotten your-self into a bit of trouble, but everything is going to work out just fine. What you saw yesterday in the woods was not what you thought it was. But it was something very profound, and because of it, your life will never be the same."

✧CHAPTER 4✧

Nothing

I don't know if profound was the best word to use, but there was no doubt that my life was about to change. Mostly for the worse.

After the voice spoke from the darkness, a small light switched on in the middle of that huge room. It was a lamp sitting on a large wooden desk. Behind the desk, propped on a cushy leather chair, sat a man that made the monster look like your neighborhood barber. It had nothing to do with their size. The man at the desk was a lot smaller than the villain who had led me to the library. But his face looked as mean as a snake. He had thin eyebrows, a skinny, pointy nose, jawbones that were about to poke through the skin, and eyes that were black as tar. His hair was gray, and he wore a fancy suit, similar to the one worn by the Monster. After looking at him and those evil eyes, I had second thoughts about my earlier conclusion that Mayor Duck was the devil. If the devil was human, he was sitting right in front of me.

I'd like to think at that point I could have acted brave, and made that mean son of a gun see that I wasn't someone to be toyed with. But all I could get my poor soul to say was, "Sir, I don't know what the heck's going on, but I'm downright scared, and I want to go home."

"Go home?" His raspy voice spoke again—I wanted to tell him to clear his throat or something. "Well, I don't really think you'll be going home anytime soon, son. You see, what you saw yesterday is a lot bigger than you may think. That woman you . . . saw . . . had been spying on us, Jimmy. Do you know what happens to spies?"

He paused, expecting me to answer, but I was too scared to even shake my head.

"Nothing good," he continued. "She found out a lot more than she bargained for, and then went way too far when she decided to take a walk in those woods to look for something that is very special to all of us. It must have been a shock for you to see your own mayor hurting that poor lady, eh?" The sicko let out a little chuckle, then continued, "You know what, son? She's now in a place that you've never even imagined in your wildest kiddy dreams. And . . . 'she ain't coming back,' as you might say. And you know what else?"

I swallowed.

"No, sir."

"If you don't do exactly what we tell you, you're going to join her."

✧ ✧ ✧

An hour later, I knew what it was that they wanted me to do.

Nothing.

It took them an hour to tell me that, but that was the message. I was supposed to sit tight and wait for them to decide what they were going to do with me. They told me if I so much as breathed wrong they'd kill me with about as much thought as stepping on a cockroach, which made me feel pretty down right special.

As they had sat there and discussed the future of a little brat named Jimmy Fincher who had stumbled upon them at their worst, I heard little bits and pieces of their conversation. They talked about my dad a lot, and some guy named

Joseph, who they had no idea how to find. They also mentioned a couple of things that really made me think they were whacked in the brain. They kept talking about opening some door before someone else did, and how they had to stop the "Givers." I had no earthly idea what they were talking about.

I was led back to my room after learning nothing of value, told to stay put and keep quiet, and then locked in. Of course, I tried the door, but it seemed pretty set in not letting me out. I also checked out the window, but it was bolted down. Even if it hadn't been, I was on at least the third floor of this mansion, and it would have been a mighty fall to jump out that window. I'd had enough jumps for one summer.

I sat on the bed and bawled my eyes out 'til there was no water left in my head. But then, I vowed I wouldn't do it again. I figured if I was old enough to get kidnapped and threatened with my life, I was old enough to quit crying.

After an hour or so, with nothing new happening, I fell back asleep. All I dreamed about was that poor woman who had her life taken away from her. And about the darkness that had sucked her away into thin air like a bad magic trick.

My world had become strange and terrifying.

It was only the beginning.

✧Chapter 5✧

Escape to Nowhere

I lived in that room for two days, with nothing to keep me company but a bed and a bolted-down window. It seemed like a whole lifetime. I had plenty of food brought to me, fresh clothes, even fresh sheets. They even let me shower, which was nice, because I had started to stink something awful, even by my standards. But I was purely miserable. I kept my word and didn't cry, but I came awfully close. All I could think about was my mom and dad and brother and friends and how much I wanted to go swimming. Every minute that went by was longer than the one before it. It wasn't too long before I started to feel crazy. Anything but that room, that bed, that window that untruthfully promised there was normal life on the other side. I hated it.

Two days.

But after two days, the waiting ended.

One morning, the Monster came into my room—without knocking, he never knocked—and said that we were going on a trip. He threw me some fresh clothes, grunted, and declared that we were leaving in five minutes. He left, leaving the door open.

I got dressed as quickly as I could, thankfully finding my Braves hat still intact and with the clothes the Monster had given me, and waited for him to come back and get me. Ten minutes went by with no sign of that ugly beast. I decided that maybe I was supposed to come downstairs on my own.

I went to the door, and peeked around the siding. The hall was empty.

I left the room and walked down the hall, on top of that plush carpet, and headed for the huge staircase that led down to the foyer, then looked down.

No one.

I went down the stairs, finally getting a good view of what this place looked like. It belonged on 'Lifestyles of the Rich and Famous.' Everywhere you looked, there was shiny gold or silver or expensive wood or lush carpet or oriental rugs—you name it, it seemed to have it. I was definitely in a bona fide mansion.

When I reached the bottom, I plopped down and sat on the bottom stair.

And waited.

Still, no sign of the Monster, or of the old devil with the raspy voice.

I waited longer still.

Finally, the passing time making me braver, I got up and started walking around the house. You sure could get lost in a mansion if you weren't careful. I walked through a couple of connected rooms, and then heard voices from somewhere to the right side of the room. If my sense of direction was correct, it would have been the room I visited during my first encounter with Raspy-voice. At the very back of the room I was currently in, a door led into the direction the voices were coming from. I could hear that raspy voice, and I knew the source immediately.

"Fine. Go get the boy, and let's do it. His father will have no choice now. That letter leaves no doubt that he knows where Joseph is hiding out. It's time to get nasty because we are running out of time. The Givers will get desperate, and may not just sit back any longer. They and their stupid legend and heroics."

Not knowing what to do, I crept behind a couch and strained to hear what I could.

"The boy!" This was the voice of the Monster. "I forgot all about him. He's up in the room with the door wide open." This was followed by a thundering of footsteps that I could tell were going out of the adjacent room through the door right next to the staircase on the other side.

I don't know how or what came over me, but I knew that my only chance in the world of seeing another day was to somehow run for it. I dashed back into the hallway, headed straight through the foyer and out the front door. A blast of sunlight hit me, and I could barely make out the humongous yard that lay before me. To the right was a cobblestone drive-way that made its way through some gardens before disappearing around a bend. In front of me was a vast expanse of green, green grass. And to my left, not more than fifty feet away, were woods.

I ran for it.

By the time I had reached the first trees, I could hear the Monster bellowing from the house, "He's gone! The little brat is gone!"

✧ ✧ ✧

I ran and ran. My heart beat as fast as it could. The trees got thicker and thicker, limbs and leaves slapping me every which way. I stumbled, and got right back up. I knew I was running for my life.

In the distance behind me, I could hear sounds of pursuit. It was faint, but someone was running through the woods behind me. Twigs breaking, leaves crackling—someone was making chase, and I was pretty sure they were catching up. My body cursed me, begged me to stop. But then the Monster would roast me like a chicken. So I ran on.

I heard a yell from behind.

"Where you going, boy? You think you can run? You're going to be dead in five minutes!"

The Monster was catching up. I *was* going to die.

Suddenly, looming before me stood a wooden fence, running in both directions for as far as I could see. There was nowhere to go. I stopped running and looked around, desperate for a solution. The fence stood at least ten feet high, so I couldn't jump it. My instincts saved me. I started climbing the same thing that had gotten me into this mess in the first place. A tree.

It was only a few feet from the fence, and I knew I could climb out on a branch and jump over from there. Sweat was pouring down my face, and I felt like I was about to collapse.

I climbed on.

I reached a big, thick branch that stooped right over that blasted fence. I was almost there. I was almost to freedom. I started climbing out onto the limb and then his voice froze me.

Panting, somehow the Monster got out some words.

"Stop right there you little good-for-nothing, or I'll make sure you never see another day in your life."

I slowly looked down and saw the barrel of a pistol—one of those fancy kind you see in FBI movies. Fear gripped me. My mind emptied of thought, my heart emptied of feelings. All I knew was fear, and I could not move.

Monster glared at me, finally catching his breath. "Now, just climb on back down here, and quit being silly. You have no idea what it is you're messing with, boy. Come back with me, and maybe you'll live another day or two." He grinned a wicked smile, and his eyes became points of evil light.

I had no choice but to obey. The last time I checked, I wasn't faster than a speeding bullet. Carefully, to make sure he didn't think I was going to do something crazy, I slowly started making my way down the tree.

When I got to a point where I was about five feet above him, I lost my mind completely. Thinking that surely this would be my last act in life, I jumped out toward the closest limb, grabbed it with my hands like a gymnast doing the parallel bars, and with every ounce of strength that existed in my little runt of a body, I kicked my foot out right into the Monster's face. I could feel his nose crunch as I connected, dead on.

He was stunned, dropping his gun as he fell to the ground. I only had seconds, and even though I was just about drained of any energy whatsoever, I shot back up to the overhanging limb, clambered out over the fence, and for the second time in three days, I jumped out of a tree.

✧CHAPTER 6✧

Stinky Old Car

Twenty minutes later, I was still running. Where that energy came from, I don't know. Pure adrenaline maybe. Whatever it was, it had saved my life for the time being. I had lost any sign of pursuit.

I was still in a wooded area, even thicker than the woods by the house I had just escaped from. Not knowing which direction was which, I just kept going, trotting now instead of full-on running. There was no sign of the Monster. Maybe I had hurt the man enough that he didn't even run after me over the fence. Or maybe he just assumed he could catch up to me later. Or, maybe they didn't think I was much of a threat after all.

I finally decided to sit down and take a rest. Exhaustion filled me as my thoughts started running with the wind.

It all seemed impossible. I was a bona fide murder-witness, kidnap-victim, hostage, and escapee all rolled into one. It was too much for me to bear. It didn't seem real. For the first time, I broke my vow, and cried. My chest lurched with sobs, the tears flowed off my face and onto my shirt, as the events of the last couple of days finally caught up with me and hit me like a blast from a shotgun. I felt so lonely.

I hated the men that did this to me.

The Monster, Raspy-voice, and Mayor Duck.

Again, I felt the rage that I had felt on the tree after seeing the Mayor kill that woman. I felt the rage that had visited me more than once while I sat in that prison of a room for two days.

I promised myself that it wasn't over.

When I finally got back to my mom and dad, I'd make sure someone important heard about the things I'd seen and been through.

✧ ✧ ✧

I hiked for another hour or so and finally came upon some civilization. It was getting toward late afternoon, and my body hurt like nothing else. Hunger pains raked me all over. I needed some help soon, or I would probably just fall down and die.

I came out of the woods onto a stretch of highway, a four-lane state road from the looks of it. There was a gas station about fifty yards down the road. Finally, I felt a little spark of hope.

I dragged myself to the station and found a phone. Having seen that stupid 'call-collect' commercial over a million times, I knew exactly how to make a call without money. My brother Rusty answered.

"Oh my—hold on, Jimmy!" he yelled.

Two seconds later my dad was on the phone.

I expected exclamations of joy, yelps of excitement, laughter and tears. All I got was a scared, trembling voice. My dad was obviously shaken.

"Where are you," he said, more of a statement than a question. His voice was low, stern, and full of fear. Why wasn't he excited? Then a thought came to me. They probably thought I was still with the kidnappers, that this was a call for ransom-demands or something.

"Dad, I escaped, I'm okay! I'm at a gas station, ummm, a Texaco."

His reply was in the same voice. "Son, I need to know

exactly where you are, and now."

"Hold on," I said, and put the phone down while I ran into the store. The surprised man at the counter let me know that I was in Buford, about a mile north of the high school, on Buford Highway. I ran back to the phone and told my dad.

"Son, walk south about a quarter of a mile. Hide in the woods until you see me pull off the road. Then run for my car and get in."

"But—"

"Just do it." He hung up.

I was stunned. That wasn't my dad's normal voice. I'd never heard him sound scared in all my life. What I'd been through was horrible at best, but I was free, it was over. Why didn't he sound happy? Why was he still so scared? Something was wrong.

After hanging up, I did as I was told and ran a little ways down the road and hid behind a tree. I figured my house couldn't be more than twenty minutes away, so I sat down and waited. My earlier loneliness, anger, and fear had subsided a bit, but now I was flooded with a whole new pile of worries. My dad. Scared. Did he know something about the people that kidnapped me? Had they talked to him? Did they know I'd be going home, figuring they could come after me there? Was that why my dad was so scared?

The questions flooded my head.

I looked up at the tree I crouched under. *Perfect for climbing*, I thought. Memories of the Mayor and that woman filled my vision, causing me to feel nauseous.

I couldn't wait to see my dad.

✧ ✧ ✧

Fifteen minutes later, he pulled up in his Isuzu I-Mark. The puke-yellow color went well with the nasty diesel fumes coming out of the exhaust. I couldn't quite see my dad through the windshield, but somehow I could sense that he was a worried mess.

I took off for the car. As soon as Dad got sight of me he reached over and pushed open the passenger-side door. I got in and closed the door.

No hug, no words like, "Happy to see ya, son!" Dad just put the car into first gear, did a U-ie, and took off, heading south, back toward home. He looked a mess. His black hair was rustled, his face unshaven, his shirt sweaty and wrinkled. His eyes were bloodshot, and huge bags had formed under them. *Goodness*, I thought, *Dad hasn't slept since I was kidnapped*. After a long silence, I finally spoke.

"Dad, what's wrong? I thought everything would be okay now." It occurred to me how strange it was that he hadn't even asked me any details about who had kidnapped me or anything.

"Son, I—" He faltered, paused, and then continued. "The people who took you, they called me right before you did. You have no idea, son. Look, I don't know how to explain things right now. But . . . son . . ."

"Dad, what?"

For the first time, he looked over at me. His eyes were filled with a grief that I would've thought impossible.

"Son . . . I've gotta get you away from this place; as far away as possible."

CHAPTER 7

Far Away

I couldn't say a word for the longest time. After Dad drove right past the turn-off to go to our house, I knew he wasn't kidding. He got on I-85, and headed south.

After a while, Dad finally started talking again.

"Okay, listen. I don't expect you to understand, and I *do* expect you to be confused and terrified. Son, this is crazy to be saying stuff like this to you, but I don't want you to underestimate what it is we're dealing with. The fact that you escaped from those hoodlums means nothing. You hear me—it means nothing! If anything, you've made matters worse. I don't even know where or how to begin."

Dad's face was flushed red, and I knew he wanted to curse. But my dad never cursed.

We were in the middle of downtown Atlanta now, and he kept going. The skyscrapers loomed over us as we drove through, the late afternoon sun glimmering off the windows of the tallest buildings. I had always loved driving through Atlanta, but now it was nothing. My insides hurt with a mixture of worry, fear, nervousness, and despair. I had never felt this way in my life. What was going on? Where was Dad taking me? The tears came again.

"Ah, son . . ." Dad said in an attempt to make his voice softer and less anxious. A very bad attempt. "Look, I have no choice but to do what I'm about to do. We're going to the airport. I'm putting you on a plane, and you're leaving us for a while, okay? I would say don't be scared, but that would be plain stupid. Be scared, Jimmy, that's the only way we're going to survive this."

My heart went through my throat, and I couldn't speak. The tears stopped swiftly, my emotions of despair replaced by a stark uncertainty. The airport? Sending me somewhere? What in the world?

"Dad, what . . . why can't we just go to the police? Who are these people? How do they know who you are? What's going on, Dad?" My voice trembled with some kind of night-marish version of Christmas morning excitement.

"Jimmy, we're almost to the airport, and I just don't have the time to explain everything right now. It goes all the way back to when I was a kid. Those people that had you—they . . . know me very well. The fact that you saw whatever it was you saw, sheez, that is a coincidence beyond all coinci-dences. I thought those people were in my past for good, but not anymore. It's started all over again. Those people are into something very strange, Jimmy, and I was right in the middle of it. I got out somehow, I thought, but . . ."

Not a word he was saying made a bit of sense.

"Jimmy, you'll understand soon enough. I'm sending you to a friend, and he'll be able to explain everything. His name is Joseph. Our only hope is that I can get back to the house before they arrive, and convince them that I don't know where you are. I hope they think you just died in those woods or something. If I can somehow make them think you're nowhere to be found, we just might be okay. They don't want any more trouble than they have to deal with. But if they know you're out there, they won't stop 'til you're dead." He looked at me again.

"That's harsh son, too much for a kid like you to have to hear, but I *cannot afford* to mince words with you. You *must* understand the gravity of our situation. They will kill you, they will kill me, they will kill our whole family if they have to. You accept that right now."

His voice had grown harsh. I was still in a daze. Things were so crazy that I was beyond any kind of rational response. I just grunted and tried to grasp everything I was hearing. I couldn't. Not then anyhow. My head was swimming.

Soon we screeched to a stop in a parking spot at the airport. Dad jumped out of the car, yelling at me to hurry up. He opened the trunk, and took out a small backpack.

"Mom put just a couple of changes of clothes in here, and some of your bathroom stuff." He opened it and pulled out a little black money purse—one of those things that's about the size of half a notebook and has a zipper all the way across the top. It was packed full.

"There's five thousand dollars in here, Jimmy. I know you've never held more than ten bucks in your life, but I don't want to take any chances. You may need it, you may need more, I don't know. You just hold on to this with your life, you hear me?"

"Yes, sir." I couldn't believe that I was about to be the richest kid in America.

"Come on," Dad said, already booking for the entrance to the terminal.

He turned around and yelled at me to hurry, and I followed, with the strangest thought that Dad's facial expression right then kind of reminded me of the Monster.

✧ ✧ ✧

When I was twelve, my family had traveled to Mexico for a little family vacation. It was hot, muggy, and miserable. Not a one of us had any fun, but at least because of that trip, I had a passport, which made it easier for Dad to get me a ticket and on the plane. From all the movies I'd seen, though, I couldn't help but think how easy it would be for the bad guys to track me down if they even suspected that I'd flown somewhere. The ticket was in my name, and obviously they knew exactly who I was. I tried to put the worry aside, but it kept nagging at me.

"Dad," I asked as we walked to the gate, "What if they come looking to see if I bought a plane ticket?"

"Then I guess they'll follow you. I don't know, son, we just gotta do the best we can." He sounded very irritated now, so I thought it best just to keep to myself for the time being.

As we walked on, I finally had time to think for just a minute. All this couldn't possibly be happening. It seemed absurd that I was actually going along with my dad's plans, actually walking with him to the gate, actually running from a bunch of hard criminals. I should've gone crazy by now, or concluded my dad was crazy, or something. It just seemed unreal that I was involved in some kind of big scandal, and about to run off to another part of the country. A week ago I was waking up at noon, swimming and climbing trees all day, watching T.V., going to the movies, or just sitting on my butt waiting for nothing. Now, I was running for my life. Go figure.

When we got to the gate, they were already loading the plane. I looked up at the message board.

ATLANTA TO SALT LAKE CITY, DEPARTURE 6:08 PM

Salt Lake City, Utah. Who would've thought that little Jimmy-boy would be going to the land of the Mormons. My best friend Tyler's family was Mormon, so I knew a lot about them. I was pretty sure I could feel safe there, as long as I didn't threaten anyone with caffeine or something.

"All right, Jimmy, you better get on. Remember, hold on to that backpack with your life. You lose that money, and you might get a little hungry." Was that a mild joke by Dad?

"Now, I mentioned Joseph earlier. He is a very dear friend to your mom and me. He lives somewhere out there in Utah—I don't even know where exactly. But I guess he figured that was the safest place for him to hide."

"Okay, Dad, but I don't even know what to say—I'm really scared. What am I supposed to do out there? And when am I going to see you guys again? What's going to happen?"

"I don't have a good answer, I guess. I promise Joseph will take care of you. He's an interesting guy ... I think you'll be a little surprised. Anyway, I love you so much son." He grabbed me and gave me one of his bear-hugs. "I'll be praying for you. Somehow, this will all work out. Now, get on that plane. You'll hear from me before too long, okay?"

He gave me a little nudge toward the loading gate, and told me to grow up and be a man now. The tears flowed down my face, and that was expected, but when I looked up and saw my dad crying, I was shocked. While my mom cried just for telling her that dinner tasted good, my dad *never* cried. I had never felt so much love from him, and it made me feel like a king. At least for that instant, I forgot all about the danger we were in. I forgot about the murder, the room, the Monster, Raspy-voice, and the chase. All I felt was the love of my dad and family, and I couldn't help but feel that we were going to make it somehow. I felt a renewed determination to help get us through this, to help save my family. I didn't know what a punk kid like me could do, but I would figure it out, and I would do it. For Dad. For Mom. For Rusty.

So with those last words and thoughts, it was time to go. I turned and practically ran onto the plane, yelling to my dad, finally able to sputter some words out, that I loved him, and that I would miss him.

And then he was gone, and I, along with my backpack, five thousand dollars, and my lucky Braves hat, was bound for Salt Lake City, Utah.

✧CHAPTER 8✧

Bald Guy

I sat in a window seat, which usually made me happy, but of course I was right over a wing, and couldn't see a thing to save my life. I thought to myself how fun it would be to look at that ugly gray thing the whole trip.

I could have put the backpack Dad had given me in the overhead thing or under my seat, but I held it in my lap instead. There was no way I was going to chance losing all that money. I felt so paranoid about it, I thought everyone who even looked my way had somehow figured out what I was carrying.

The plane was a big one—that's about all I could do to describe it. I didn't know if it was a 747 or what, but it had two seats going down the sides, and five going down the middle. I sure was glad I wasn't in a middle seat in the middle section. I would've died.

After a little delay, we finally took off for Salt Lake City. For some reason, I almost felt excited. All the fear and sadness had just kind of left me, I guess, and I was excited to see what I'd find in Utah. But deep down, I felt the slight panicky feeling that my excitement would not last long, that it was only a temporary relief from all the anguish I'd been experiencing.

I thought about everything that my dad had told me, and tried to piece it all together. Something about Raspy and them being into something strange, and that my dad had been a part of it. Raspy had mentioned my dad several times in the mansion, but I never really knew why. So somehow my dad was connected to these nutcases. I couldn't possibly imagine how.

The best I could come up with was that a long time ago, my dad had been involved in or somehow knew about things that Monster and Raspy were doing. The Mayor, too. Maybe Dad had sworn he would never tell anyone, and everything was okay until my unfortunate meeting with Mayor Duck. Dad had said it was an incredible coincidence. So the facts that I'm Dad's son, and that I just happened to see something I shouldn't have, and that what I saw is somehow linked to my dad, has gotten him back into his original mess. Whatever. Something told me that I had only scratched the surface, and that big surprises lay ahead.

The stewardess announced that a movie would be shown, some lovey-dovey flick that I wouldn't have seen in a million years by my own choice, but I figured there wasn't anything else to do, so I decided I'd watch. I pulled open my backpack to get out some money, being careful so as not to let anyone know about my riches. I unzipped the little purse and pulled out a bill. I just about choked when I saw the "100." *Well,* I thought, *forget the movie.* I wasn't about to hand that lady a hundred dollar bill for a dinky set of headphones. I could just imagine the attention I'd get while she counted out ninety-four dollars of change.

So instead, I took a little nap. After the last day of non-stop running from bad guys, I felt a bit tired.

✧ ✧ ✧

I must have missed the nasty dinner, because when I woke up, my ears already felt like they were stuffed with cheese or something, and we were getting close to landing. It had also grown dark, despite the fact that we were flying west.

When I came to my senses, all the calm and peace I had felt earlier left as quick as it had come. I was scared to death all over again. What was I going to do when I got off the plane? How was I supposed to know who this Joseph character was? What if he wasn't there at all? Dad had said he was a bit unusual—what if he was psycho or something? How long had it been since my dad had seen this guy? Question after question, but no answers yet.

The plane landed—without crashing thank goodness—and it was time to get off. Gripping my bag like my life depended on it, I slowly made my way down the aisle with the rest of the impatient folks, walked down the thing that connects the plane to the terminal building, and stepped into the Salt Lake airport.

There was a mass of airport chairs, people, kids, strollers, wheelchairs, luggage, newspapers, security guards, huge windows—definitely an airport. But as soon as I stepped off that plane, my eyes focused on the strangest person I might've ever seen.

Twenty feet away stood a man, tall as a tree, with not a hair on his head. His skin looked pale, and he had very distinct features—sharp, blue eyes, a somewhat-pointed nose, ears that stuck out like they were trying to escape, and a ragged jaw-line. His chin was rounded, and he had a big dimple right under his lips. His neck was long, but muscular, and the rest of his body was bulky, not completely hidden by the clothes he wore—if his horrendous outfit could be classified as clothes. Puke-green T-shirt that was just a little too small, red jeans that barely made it to his ankles, no socks, and orange flip-flops. As strange as he appeared, something about this man was eerily comforting and reassuring.

I had no doubt as to whom I was looking at.

Joseph.

✧CHAPTER 9✧
Strange Photos

"Hello, Jimmy."

His voice was whispery and soft, almost hard to hear. It seemed downright eerie.

"Hey. I guess you're the guy my dad was talking about—Joseph," I replied.

"Yes, I am. I reckon your dad thinks I can save you from the Union of Knights, but I've got my doubts about that one. Well, now," he said, seeing my look of puzzlement, "you haven't got a clue what's going on, do you?"

If I had thought this guy strange from his looks, it was all more than confirmed after thirty seconds of talking to him. Union of Knights? This guy wasn't chopping with a full hatchet.

"Actually, sir, I don't. Dad told me very little before he got me on that plane. Something about the past, and him getting out of something bad, but that's it." I had the sudden thought that I was trusting this guy too soon, making too many assumptions.

He lightly touched my arm, and suggested that we get out of the airport and go somewhere else. Alarms went off in my head.

"Well, I don't know. I, uh, don't even know you. I don't know if I should just go running around with a stranger. Uh . . . let me call my dad." My voice shook.

"No, no, no—that's impossible. THEY might be at your

house, waiting to answer the phone. No, it's time to take every possible precaution. But I can understand your hesitancy. I will prove my loyalty to you and your dad if you'll just follow me to my car. It's in a lighted area right next to the doors to the ticketing area." He gave me a smile, and it was pretty genuine. "Okey-dokey-smokey?"

I hate it when people say that.

"All right. I'll at least do that much." Like I had anything else to do. What would I do, go rent a car and get me a hotel room? He turned and started walking, and I followed.

We passed a million people, all looking like they were in some world of a hurry. I don't know what it is about airports, but I love walking around in them. Maybe it's because I think airplanes are so cool, and I like to look at weirdos. It can't seem possible, but every time I've been in an airport, my family and I seemed to be the only normal ones in the whole place.

We were heading past a food court, making our way to the escalators, when Joseph spoke again.

"Jimmy, you hungry? Want a burger or something?"

I was starving, having missed the lovely airplane food. But I felt anxious to find out what Joseph's "proof" was. "No," I said, "Let's go ahead and go to your car."

The car fit the person. It was an old VW Bug, with the worst paint job I'd ever seen—an assortment of grays, blues, and white, all patched together in little haphazard shapes. I couldn't tell if it was deliberate or if the previous paint jobs were showing through the current one.

Joseph popped open the trunk, which was in the front—a thing I've never understood about those cars—and pulled out a couple of big books. At first I couldn't tell what they were, but when he put them in front of me, I could see that they were photo albums. He wanted to show me pictures of himself to prove he was safe?

I wasn't ready for what the albums contained.

There must have been a million pictures inside, and they were all of Joseph—with all the people that were a part of my life. There was a picture of him at our dinner table, laughing with my mom. A picture of him in a three-legged race with my mom as his partner. A picture of him wrestling with Rusty in our living room. A picture of him putting up Christmas lights on our house. A picture of Joseph in front of the Duluth City Hall, with Mayor Duck—that one made me a little nervous. A picture of Joseph throwing a football in the front yard of my house—the house I had lived in since the day I was born.

A picture of Joseph reading a book to a small boy in his lap.

The boy was me.

"You see, Jimmy, I think it's pretty fair to say that you can trust me. I reckon you can trust me a lot more than you think." Joseph had put on a very serious face, and his eyes bore into me like a hot iron.

"Yeah, I guess so. Well . . . how come I don't remember you at all? I mean, if you were so close to our family, how come I've never even heard of you?"

Joseph winked at me, and said, "All in good time, Jimmy."

As I relented, got in the car, and drove off with him, a thought popped in my head with a force that almost made me jump out of my seat.

In all those pictures, not a single one had my dad in it.

✧CHAPTER 10✧

Short Friendship

We drove for quite some time, in complete silence, heading toward a big shadowy horizon that I figured were mountains. I'd never seen mountains before, at least not the rocky kind, and actually looked forward to seeing them the next day when it was light outside. Joseph pulled off at an exit that said something about ski resorts, and we were soon climbing a steep, curvy road. I finally broke the silence with the question that had been burning in my mind.

"Joseph, why wasn't my dad in any of those pictures you showed me?"

He hesitated, and I knew something was fishy about the whole thing.

"You're very observant, Jimmy," he said, and I thought it was pretty dumb to call it observant—it seemed obvious. He continued, "That's a long story. I'll catch you up later on the whole mess. But not here. Man, I didn't think about that. I promise I could've brought others that *did* have your dad in them."

I was fed up.

"C'mon, I'm sick of you and my dad telling me to wait, that I'll soon know everything. Just tell me. How did you know my family?"

"I grew up in Duluth, that's how. Your grandfather and my father were . . . close. They were part of a group that started something called the Union of Knights. I know it sounds like some dumb fantasy novel, but it isn't anything like that. That's just a name they pulled out of the air, and I guess they thought it was pretty cool. Kind of stupid, huh?"

"Yeah," was my only reply, trying to relay the point that I wanted him to continue.

"Anyway, this . . . club . . . was something quite extraordinary. It wasn't like the Boy Scouts or the Lion's Club, it was . . ." he trailed off, looking into his rear-view mirror like someone was following us. I looked back over my shoulder and saw a car about 50 yards behind us, gaining speed. My nerves jumped in alarm.

But the car caught up with us quickly and just passed on by. *Man*, I thought, *aren't they in a hurry.*

"You were saying?" I prodded.

"Yeah, uh. . ." Beads of sweat covered his brow, and his eyes showed traces of fear. "Yeah, anyway, this club I was telling you about. Like I said, it was quite a unique gathering of people. Every last one of them was crazy—so crazy as to scare the willies out of the bravest soul. You won't believe it, Jimmy. They were just plain and simply *insane*. I'll admit they found something pretty incredible after all their searching, but they're still psychotic. And that's why they are the scariest people I've ever come across. I hate to have to be the one to tell you about your ancestry like this, but like you said, it's time to quit beating around the bush."

He pulled off onto a little dirt road, and we drove up a very steep incline until we stopped in a small driveway of what looked like some kind of old log cabin. There wasn't a light in sight but for the headlights of the car. The woods surrounding the cabin seemed like walls of wood, shutting us in from the rest of the world. I suddenly felt claustrophobic.

"We're here!" Joseph said, a little too cheerfully for the circumstances.

"Where's here?" I asked.

"We're in Alta Canyon, at a cabin that I bought about ten years ago—a place that I felt like I could come and hide from . . . the world every once in a while."

"I thought Utah was supposed to be a place where they wouldn't suspect us? What if they come here looking for us?" I wondered why it seemed like I was the smarter of the two sitting in that car.

"Nonsense. It's not like those people are that smart, Jimmy. You think they're the mafia or something? Now come on." I had the feeling he didn't believe his own words.

He jumped out of the car, leaving it running, and walked up to some kind of electrical box. A couple of switches later and we had some outside lights on, making everything seem a little safer.

Joseph returned and turned off the car. With a little apprehension, I got out of the car as well. I still wasn't too sure about this guy. I clutched my bag, and waited to follow him into the cabin. I heard a twig break somewhere out in the woods, and the skin on the back of my neck shot straight up.

"Did you hear that?" I asked, embarrassed at how scared my voice sounded.

"Yeah. Here, open that door and go inside. I already unlocked it." He pointed to a door halfway in the shadows, on the left side of the cabin. I didn't recall him unlocking it.

The door opened easily. I stepped inside and looked around. All I could see were faint shadows, the only light being that which spilled in from outside. I groped along the wall for a light switch, but only found a nice splinter that made me wince in pain. So I stood and waited, either for Joseph or for my eyes to adjust. Without warning, the outside lights turned off. I gasped, and crouched down onto my knees.

Ten seconds of silence followed—an eternity.

Then the air rocked with the sudden sound of an explosion so loud that it made my eardrums feel like they had shattered. Acting on some kind of instinct, I threw myself flat onto the floor, waiting for the whole cabin to come collapsing down on top of me. But then I realized it was from outside—was it a shotgun blast? Dynamite? I didn't know enough about any of that stuff to make an educated guess. But something bad had just happened.

A few seconds later, someone stumbled through the doorway and crashed onto the floor, not more than three feet away from me.

"Jimmy . . ."

It was Joseph, struggling to even speak.

"Jimmy . . ."

He pulled something out from under him—a flashlight, and flicked it on.

I stared.

He was covered in blood—his face, his neck, his clothes. I couldn't tell where the wound was, or if there was even a single wound at all. He just looked like he had jumped in a river of red paint. Who had done this to him?

"Jimmy . . . he's still out there . . . listen to me." He could barely get the words out. "Remember these three words. *Old . . . Willow's . . . Trunk*. That's where it is. And trust no one, Jimmy, no one but your father. Even I don't know who's on whose side. *Old Willow's Trunk*. DO . . . NOT . . . FORGET . . . IT! The . . . key . . ."

His voice faded into death with one last gasp.

Joseph, the man who was supposed to take care of me, the only bead of hope in a string of fear and despair, the one who was going to finally answer all my questions, was gone.

And I was alone, in a cabin, not knowing what was beyond the door, waiting out there in the darkness.

✧Chapter 11✧

Hairy

Scared to death, I picked up the flashlight and turned it off. I figured if someone were still out there, I didn't want to let them know exactly where I was. Let us both be in darkness—at least then we're on even terms.

I scooted over to the wall directly beside the front door, and waited for a few minutes. I couldn't hear a sound coming from anywhere, except for normal nighttime sounds like crickets and hooting owls. Had the person run off? What had happened? Joseph looked like someone had set off a bomb right under his nose, but I didn't think the noise had been loud enough to be anything like that. I concluded that someone must have used a shotgun or something. So where was he, or she, now?

No, Joseph had said "he," I thought. That meant that they had interacted at least briefly before the gun was shot. The way Joseph had said "he's still out there"—something about his tone made it sound like Joseph had known the man.

After a few minutes of running through these thoughts in my head, I decided to take a peek outside. My confidence was building that the man had done his business and taken off. But why would he have left me there?

I peeked around the edge of the door, crouched on my hands and knees.

Nothing but shadows, caused by the faint moonlight.

I decided that this guy might just be sitting there, waiting for me to get relaxed, so that he could jump me. If that were the case, then he must want me alive, I thought, because if he had a shotgun, it didn't really matter what state I was in.

I had to do something.

I groped around the floor, looking for a hard object. A few feet from the door was a bookshelf, and I grabbed a nice big book. I looked around the cabin, and spotted a window in the middle of the back wall. Holding the book like a Frisbee, I swung it as hard as I could toward the window, and the book was true to my aim. The crashing sound as it broke through the window and into the woods was like a freight train compared to the silence that had preceded it.

Hoping that the bad guy was dumb enough to think that I was dumb enough to jump out of a window without knowing what lay below, I waited a couple of seconds and then took off out the front door. I had the flashlight in my hands, turned off, but nothing else. I didn't look to the left or right, I just ran straight ahead.

Straight ahead into a massive body, causing me to fall right back down onto the ground.

My head hit a rock, and everything went black.

My plan hadn't worked too well.

✧ ✧ ✧

When I woke up, I was lying on the floor, with morning sunshine coming through a nearby window. I could tell that I wasn't in the cabin anymore, but rather in what looked like a motel or something. The stuff that had happened the night before came rushing back into my brain, and I went into a panic. I jumped up and looked at the bed in the room, and sure enough there was someone sleeping there, snoring like a stuffy-nosed pig. It had to be the truck of a man that I had run into last night, guessing from the size of the gigantic lump under the covers.

Not in the mood to hang out with the fella, I slowly crept toward the door. But one of my legs didn't want to cooperate, and I looked down and saw that it was chained to the dresser handle. *Dang it*, I thought, *what in all get out is going on here?*

"Now, now, there little buddy, you ain't got no plans on leaving do ya?"

The deep voice came from the whale under the sheets, and I couldn't do a thing but look his way. His big head poked out of the covers, and he grinned right at me. My heart froze in fear—not for the first time in the last little while.

"Sir, I'm real scared and I don't have any idea what's going on here. Please just let me go and I swear on my scrawny little life I won't rat on anybody or anything I've seen. I swear, sir—please, let me go."

The man threw off the covers and slowly rolled up into a sitting position. I almost gasped out loud—the man was so hairy he looked like Big Foot. Hair was everywhere—all over his enormous body. I couldn't help but have the odd thought right then that the man should shave that nasty stuff off if he ever went to the pool, or somebody'd think the gorillas were loose and shoot him with a tranquilizer.

"Sonny boy, you can just sit yourself down and relax. I ain't nobody you should be scared of. If it weren't for me, you'd be deader than Abraham Lincoln." He gave me another grin, and continued on when I just stared. "Jimmy, I'm Joe. I know your daddy sent you looking for me, so relax, you've found me."

I stared some more, shocked at his words. Ten seconds before I would've thought it impossible, but I was now more confused. If this was Joseph, then who was—

"What're you talking about?" I asked.

"Jimmy, that man who picked you up, he was after you, son. I was late for the airport because he or some other fool slit my tires so as they could be there to snatch you up. I took a taxi and got there just in time to follow you up to that stupid cabin. And, of course, shot that one fool dead. So, like I said, you'd be dead as dirt if it weren't for me. Any questions?"

What was I supposed to say to that?

"Well . . . how do I know you ain't the bad guy and the one you killed really was Joseph? He sure didn't seem like a bad guy to me." I was stammering now.

"I risked my life to save you."

He said it so matter-of-fact like, with a grimness to his face that kind of took me aback. I didn't know what to think, because the man who had picked me up from the airport sure didn't seem like he was out to do me harm, and all I knew of this fella was that he had killed at least one person in his life now. And those pictures I had seen—how could I argue with those? So, I did the smartest thing a little runt like myself knew how—I decided I'd play along, no matter what the truth. Joe, or no Joe, this mess of hair sitting on the bed was going to be my buddy for a while, until I knew more about the crazy road my life had suddenly decided to take a drive on. All that mattered now was finding out what all this was about, and how I could get back home.

I paused a little while, then finally said, "I believe you, I guess. So, can you tell me what's going on? I've been run after like I was the only deer in Georgia or something and I think it's about time somebody told me why." I felt certain that was the most grown-up thing I had ever said. The reply, however, was less than satisfying.

"Yeah, son, right after I take care of some business." He headed for the bathroom, a massive ball of hair with shorts on.

I slumped back onto the floor, holding back the tears, and thought of Mom, Dad, and Rusty.

✧CHAPTER 12✧

Psycho

Hair-Man finally came out of the bathroom after a good half-hour or so. I guess he decided he needed to take a shower as well before he told me anything. I had to wonder if the man used soap to clean his body or if he just went with the shampoo. And with all that hair, did he have to use conditioner, too? I hated using conditioner, but my mom said if I didn't, I'd get dandruff. Anyway, I'd had enough of the thoughts conjured up by thinking about what Hairy did in the shower.

He came over to the bed and sat down, with his towel wrapped around his furry behind. I quickly rolled over on the floor so I didn't have to witness the Beast put his clothes on. I kept waiting to hear a growl or two as he got dressed.

When he finished, he came over and kicked me gently on the back, and told me to sit up and look at him. I did as I was told.

"Jimmy, we've got a lot of talking to do, so why don't we go get us some breakfast somewhere? You up for it?" He was trying too hard to be nice, and it didn't sound very genuine, but I guessed it was better than him being mean to me.

"Yes, sir. I am pretty hungry—" Suddenly I had a thought, shutting me right up.

The money.

My bag of money from Dad.

Where could it be? Was my backpack still in Joseph's car? Did I dare ask Hairy? I decided to just ask about the backpack, as if I wanted some fresh clothes.

"Could I maybe take a shower? Did you happen to grab my pack from Jo—, I mean, whoever that was, from their car?" I hoped.

"Yeah, I grabbed it. It's over there by that chair." He pointed to an ugly blue chair, which I reckoned belonged in a motel. "Hurry and shower, 'cuz I'm 'bout to starve." He flopped down on the bed and flipped on the TV. I grabbed the backpack and practically jumped into the bathroom, closing the door shut probably just a little too anxiously. I had to make sure the money was still there.

To my relief, not a bill was missing.

Hairy hadn't taken anything out of the backpack—in fact, he'd placed the flashlight from the cabin into it, along with my Braves hat. What did that mean, I wondered. If he were a bad guy, I figured he'd for sure look through my stuff and take the money. Once again I felt as confused as a blinded squirrel with no legs.

I took a quick shower, got dressed, put on my hat, and then wondered what I should do with the money. It was too much to jam in my pockets, but I put as much as I could in them. I also did the old folded money in the sock thing. But there were still a few bills left.

Well, I reckoned, good thing I wear the tighty-whitey undies, because that's where they went.

✧ ✧ ✧

We went to a little shanky thing right next to the motel. It wasn't Waffle House, but I guess Utah doesn't have too many of those. The waitress acted really nice, and even called me honey, which I would have thought only happened in the South, but I guess I was wrong. And by the looks of the folks sitting around me, I figured hicks weren't just a southern thing either.

I ordered up a cheese omelet because they didn't have any grits. I wondered how people could get along without grits and eggs.

Hairy, who I had no choice but to call Joe—even though I didn't totally believe he really *was* Joe—sat across from me, and ate like a madman. At the rate that man was stuffing food into his mouth, I figured I would never hear the story. He finally calmed down a bit, and started talking.

"All right, Jimmy. You ready for some info? Hold onto your seat, 'cuz things ain't like you've always thought them to be. Here goes: First of all, your granddaddy was a bad man. He helped start a band of men called the—"

I cut him off.

"Union of Knights."

"Yeah. Did that fool who picked you up from the airport tell you that?"

"He sure did."

That didn't make any sense whatsoever to me. One of these men had to be a bad guy, but it looked like they might tell me the same story. Well, I figured, shut up and let the man go on.

"Well, I don't know what else he told ya, but hush up and listen. I'm sure he filled you with lies, so it's time to hear the truth. Like I was sayin,' your granddaddy helped start this group, the Union, right there in Duluth, where you was born and raised. Their original intent was just to go around robbing people and roughing up the people they didn't care for, and just doing all around no-good stuff. Well, they got bigger and a little more powerful, and it went to their heads. They thought they were the mafia or something, Jimmy. It wasn't long before murdering somebody was like making toast to those rascals. It got bad, Jimmy, real bad.

They were also into things that would give ya nightmares. I bet you didn't have the slightest clue about any of this, did ya?"

I didn't, and I was already wondering about something he'd said. I just couldn't believe that in all my life, I'd never heard one word that would tarnish the name of my grandpa. I mean, we had pictures and written-down stories of the guy. How could he have been such a man as Hairy described? I listened on, aching to finally hear some answers.

"Well, they was soon running your little town of Duluth, Georgia. And your daddy had no choice but to be sucked into it, on account he grew up around it. He's been in it for a long time, even though you don't know about it. We've gotta stop him, Jimmy. It's going to be hard for you to accept, but we've gotta stop your daddy. Now that Jo—"

He stopped, and just looked at me, waiting for me to react or something. I was so stunned, I just stared right back. I didn't know what to believe, but his words got to me. What he said about my family, especially my grandpa, just couldn't be true, just couldn't!

"What I mean to say, Jimmy," he said, "is that your daddy is the only man alive that knows where something very important is. And if he uses *that* something to get *another* something, the world as we know it will never be the same. You understand me, boy?"

Albert Einstein couldn't have understood a word this fool was talking about.

And although I was just as confused as before—if not more—at least Hairy had finally cleared up one thing for me. He'd made two big mistakes—among many little ones. First, he'd almost said Joseph's name, like an idiot, which obviously meant he wasn't Joseph. And second, and most importantly, he'd questioned my dad's character. I now knew, beyond any kind of doubt in the world, that the Hairy beast sitting in front of me was a liar to the nth degree. And a murderer.

I finally decided to speak, to humor old Hairy.

"What 'something' are you talking about?" I stammered.

He leaned closer, almost knocking down his water glass. His voice became a whisper.

"Jimmy. Your daddy knows where the key is."

The key. Old Willow's Trunk. Joseph's last words. I knew I was on the breadth of discovering something very important. My mind raced.

Joseph was the one who knew where the key was, I thought. And his last words in life were to tell me where it was. The way he told me, the desperation that had been in Joseph's last words, made me also think that there was no way my dad knew—or anyone, for that matter. His last words had been spoken in such a way as to leave no doubt that he was passing on information that must never be forgotten, or it would be lost to the world.

Funny that in the middle of all these thoughts about the key, I didn't even have the slightest clue as to what the dang *key* was, or what it opened.

"And what *something* does this key lead to?" I asked Hairy, the biggest liar I'd ever known.

"More power than you can imagine, Jimmy-boy. The power to rule the world. And not just the one we're sitting on right now."

My goodness, I thought. *Hairy isn't just a liar. He is a genuine psycho.*

✧CHAPTER 13✧

The Cruise

The next day, I found myself in a car with the hairiest man in the world, heading south on Interstate 15. We'd gone back to the motel the night before, and I'd tried my darndest to sleep, with no luck. For some reason, all the rest of that day and night, Hairy had barely spoken to me. It was like he'd realized that even the little he had told me was a stupid thing for him to do—like he realized that once again his lack of common sense had gotten the best of him.

He was right. If he was a bad guy, and I was a good guy, then he'd told me way too much. And it also looked like he'd made one whopper of a mistake killing Joseph. I also noticed that as the day had worn on, Hairy had been less and less diligent in his acting attempts. Would Joseph, the guy who had saved my life and wanted to join me in a battle against my evil father chain me to the dresser? Two nights in a row? Poor Hairy, I thought. Dumber than dirt, and as hairy as a monkey.

Then late last night, he'd gotten a phone call, and had demanded that I go into the bathroom and turn on the fan. He unlocked the chain, and I did as he said. When he let me out and chained me up again, I knew that something was terribly wrong. Hairy's whole demeanor had changed—he was no longer even attempting to be Mr. Nicey-nice.

And the next day, early in the morning, we were in a car heading south.

"Where are we going?" I asked. He'd not said a word about it yet.

"I rented a boat. Don't you think it's about time we had some fun?"

A week before that would have made me as excited as a dog in a swimming pool, but this time it only filled me with dread. Something was weird.

"Why in the world did you get a boat? Hardly seems like a time to be messing around and all."

"Lighten up, hardnose. Better to get out and do something rather than sit around waiting for nothing. Who knows when . . . your daddy's going to call and say it's all right to come home. Let's take a chill pill and go have some fun." It was like he had completely forgotten the dumb lies he'd told me the night before. Suddenly he wanted me to think we were just waiting for good ol' Dad to call so we could go home.

He smiled at me, and all it did was make me more nervous. I might not be *the* smartest kid in the world—close, maybe—but after a couple of days I could see right through this big ball of hair. He was up to something. And it wasn't good.

We drove on for I don't know how long, but it seemed like it'd never end. We drove through a canyon, then through a bunch of the ugliest land I'd ever seen. Of course, I had never seen a desert before—except on TV, but this was a lot worse than I'd have imagined it. I didn't realize that some places in the world just flat-out didn't have any trees.

We drove for miles and miles, and the ugly, boring-as-all-get-out land didn't do much in the way of helping the time go by. But after about four or five hours, Hairy pulled onto a dirt road that led to a little park with some docks leading into a big lake. I couldn't help but think that going boating could actually be fun if I weren't with a guy who had murdered one of my dad's best friends.

We got out of the car, and I just waited, leaning against the hood, while Hairy went and did the business of getting the boat. Before long, we were out in the lake, speeding along, and I tried my best to enjoy it a little bit. I went up to the front of the boat and leaned out, straight ahead. The wind tore at my hair like crazy, and my eyes watered, but it felt cool. For just a moment, I forgot all the bad stuff. For just one moment, I turned into happy little Jimmy Fincher again.

It didn't last long.

After we'd ridden along for a bit, Hairy left the thing going, straight as an arrow toward the distant side, faster than I'd ever been in a boat, and he turned towards me. I don't know much about boats, but somehow the thing could go pretty straight without his hand on the wheel.

If there had ever been even the slightest doubt in my head that Hairy was a bad guy, it dissolved pretty quickly. Out of nowhere, his face lost anything close to goodness and he grabbed me by the wrist and yanked me down onto the bottom of the boat. I cried out—more out of sudden fear than the pain in my wrist. Not only did he hurt my wrist, I hit my head on the bottom.

He yanked me back up and slapped me on the face, sending a jolt of pain through my nerves, and a wave of shock through my brain.

He threw me onto the side-seat near the back of the boat, behind the driver's seat, and chained my wrist to the little metal bar that runs along the side of the boat. This time he didn't use a chain but used some handcuffs from his bag. He picked my Braves hat off of the boat floor and threw it over the side. That made me downright ticked off.

My world was turning crazier by the minute, and I could feel the panic coming back that had just about killed me in my earlier tree and cabin adventures. My face must have shown it.

"Quit your crying, you little snotty-nose. Boy, do you have any idea how stupid you are? Just like your daddy. And old Joe. Nothing but cowards and idiots, all of ya. Well, your daddy got a little too brave this time, messing with the Sheriff. And now you're going to pay for it. I hope you've had a good life, Jimmy, cuz it's got about five minutes left in it. Dang it, why couldn't the Sheriff just come and get me himself instead of making me come all the way down here? I hate having to use the Random Rippings. I was lucky we had one close to Joseph, or I'd be dragging his poor body right along with us."

I had no idea what the fool was talking about, and he noticed my puzzled look.

"Jimmy-boy, you ain't got a clue. Just to make ya more confused, do you realize that after I get rid of you, I'll suddenly be nowhere near the state of Utah before you even hit the bottom of the lake?"

He was right—he made me more confused.

He slowed the boat down a little and started rummaging through his little pack while the wind flapped all those nasty hairs on his body this way and that. He finally found what he sought, and with his hand still in the bag, gave me a slow, evil grin. Then the hand came out.

Old Hairy was holding a gun.

✧ ✧ ✧

For twenty minutes, Hairy sat there and yapped about nothing. In all the dumb movies, the killer says to the hero that 'well, since you're going to die anyway, I might as well tell you my whole evil plan and reveal everything.' Then, of course, the hero escapes, and knows enough to foil the plan. Well, Hairy was dumber than fried eggs, but he didn't tell me any more about the whole mess behind everything. He just went on and on about how stupid my dad was and how he and Joseph had screwed everything up. And that at last he could get some payback by getting rid of little old me.

I didn't get much out of it because I was too busy panicking and trying to get out of the handcuffs somehow. It was useless.

There I was, handcuffed to the bar, sitting in the side seat, and there Hairy was, pacing around the boat, yapping about how he couldn't wait to get rid of me. I guess the only halfway good thing at that point was that Hairy had been so kind as to leave his shirt on.

It wasn't long before things changed. At the same time, we both heard the distant sound of an engine. It got louder and louder pretty quickly. And then Hairy turned white as goat's milk and revved the boat up to full speed.

I yanked my head around toward the back and saw a beautiful sight. Not far behind us was a wave runner, one of those snowmobile-for-water things, and it was a big, fast one like my Uncle Benny owns. I figured that the boat we were on wasn't anywhere near top-of-the-line, and that the wave runner was. It had a chance. But I couldn't tell who was on it.

I looked back toward the front. Hairy had left the wheel again, heading toward the back of the boat, lifting the gun as he went. Right there, in what couldn't have been more than a couple of seconds, a million thoughts went through my head.

First, there was no doubt that the boat was veering to the left, and we were almost to the other side of the lake. And sure enough, there was nothing but a huge, nasty, rocky cliff wall waiting for us. I knew that the old boat wasn't going to win that battle.

Second, I figured that the guy on the wave runner had

to be a good guy, come to save me. Why else would Hairy be so upset?

And finally, I knew that I didn't want Hairy shooting at my only hope.

I had almost forgotten the craziness that had come over me when I swung out on that limb and kicked the Monster right square in the face a couple of days ago. The willie-nillies came over me again, and I acted without thinking.

Adrenaline filled me.

I braced my left arm against the bar it was chained to, grabbed the edge of the seat with my right arm, and put every ounce of my strength into pushing down with my arms and kicking up with my legs. With both of them, straight and together, I kicked forward with all of my strength, right into the middle of Hairy's back.

Hairy lurched forward, tripped, and fell face-first onto the side of the boat. His stomach slammed onto the metal bar on that side, his legs flipped up, and he tumbled right off the boat. If I hadn't been chained to a speeding boat heading towards a rocky cliff, I would've had a good laugh at that wonderful sight.

Two things then happened that I could scarcely believe. The first is that I grabbed at the lever that controls the boat speed, and could just barely reach it. I lunged and pulled with all my strength.

The thing sprang loose and flopped back and forth like a fish. Something had obviously snapped or broken.

Talk about something that happens in dumb movies. But it did—the thing flat-out broke. And I couldn't reach the steering wheel—I had been lucky enough to reach the lever.

The second thing that happened was that I finally turned and looked at the wave runner, now forty or fifty feet behind the boat, coming up fast. And clear as the morning sun after a dry and beautiful evening, I could see the man on the wave runner, his face full of fear, anger, and unwavering determination to save his son's life.

Dad had come to save me.

✧CHAPTER 14✧

The Blackness

I wondered where in the world he had come from, and how he knew that I was in the middle of a lake five hours from Salt Lake City. But I didn't care and started screaming like crazy that I was in trouble.

I looked ahead again at the cliff face.

We were getting there fast—probably two or three minutes from crashing.

I looked back at Dad. He was getting closer and closer. It was going to be tight.

I tried not to panic, tried not to cry. It killed me that there was nothing I could do. I had yanked with all my strength on the handcuffs—no luck at all. All I could do was wait.

I looked at the cliff again. Maybe a minute and a half. Back at Dad. Twenty feet away. Ten.

Another look at the cliff.

All thoughts vanished when I saw what was now on the cliff that had not been there seconds before. My mouth went dry.

On the cliff face, right where we were heading, a ... *hole* suddenly appeared. Just a big blackness, with irregular edges, like somebody had squirted the biggest ink blot in history. It looked like somebody had hung up a piece of glass right before they squirted the ink—it was definitely flat. And the hole was darker than even the darkest ink. Right there, before the cliff. Although my life had been getting stranger by the day, this certainly topped everything else. For the life of me, I could not think of one thing to explain what I was looking at. It was just . . . empty, black, nothing. And then I realized it reminded me of that darkness I had seen when Mayor Duck had made the lady disappear.

We were heading straight for it. I didn't know which was worse—the cliff or the black ink spot.

All those thoughts went through my head in about five seconds.

I jerked my head back around to Dad, and screamed again for help.

He moved up alongside the boat now. The water rocked, and Dad kept slamming against the boat. He was trying desperately to get in a position where he could jump onto the boat and get me.

My nerves turned to ice.

Slam! He hit the boat hard and almost fell off.

Again he approached. I could see the stern determination in his eyes. I wished so badly that I could help.

He pulled up close, rocking on the waves like crazy, fighting the handle of the wave runner, keeping her steady and in line with the boat.

He gave me a desperate look, and then went for it.

He jumped, pushing himself straight towards the boat. The wave runner lurched the other direction right when he jumped, and he didn't get all the power he needed. He slammed against the side of the boat, hard, with just one arm and one leg barely draped over the ledge along the side.

He held on. His hands gripped the railing like iron, his knuckles white with strength and desperation. I could tell his body was getting slammed against the side of the boat by the rushing water. I figured we had less than a minute before we hit the cliff, or the hole, or whatever it was.

With a final feat of strength, Dad pulled himself up over the railing, slipping into the boat. He ran to me and helplessly pulled on the handcuffs. Then he ran for the steering wheel. He jerked and fiddled with the lever in vain.

He yelled out, "There's no way we can turn it in time!"

Thirty seconds. Maybe.

I just yelled out, "Help, Dad!"

His eyes focused on something.

I followed his gaze.

Hairy had dropped the gun, and it was on the floor of the boat.

Fifteen seconds.

Dad jumped forward and picked up the gun. He ran to me, and yelled to look away. An explosion ripped through the air and my arm jerked free, the handcuffs blown to oblivion. I could feel the burn of the gunshot, but there was no time to hurt.

Five seconds.

Dad grabbed me.

Two seconds.

With his arms around my waist, Dad threw the both of us off the boat.

As I fell backward, falling toward the cold water, time seemed to slow, and I caught a glimpse of the boat as it hit the black, gaping hole.

The boat completely disappeared into darkness.

No explosion, no crash.

It *disappeared.*

CHAPTER 15

Driving

My dad and I didn't say a word to each other as we swam to the wave runner, struggled to get on—we tipped it over a couple of times—and headed back the way we had come. What do people say to each other when they witness something that is absolutely impossible? Although I had barely scratched the surface of figuring out that the world I was born into is a place of wonder and the impossible, I felt stunned at what I had seen. A boat that just up and disappeared into a wall of blackness hanging in the middle of the air.

Somewhere along the way, I realized that I still had my backpack, and the money—although it was a little wet having been stuffed in my clothes and undies. But I sure missed my lucky Braves hat. I felt naked without it.

We didn't waste much time after we finally made it to the docks, dried off, and returned the wave runner to the rental place. Dad said that we were going on a road trip back home—via Omaha, Nebraska for reasons I'd soon find out—because it had obviously proven to be unsafe buying a plane ticket. We weren't totally sure that was how Raspy figured out when I'd be getting to Salt Lake—he could've just guessed I'd go to Joseph so he sent Hairy to follow him. But we were done taking chances.

Dad had rented a car, and so it was that I was on a rural highway, in the middle of Utah, heading east, with the sun having already set in the west, when I found out a whole bunch more about the background of my latest adventures. It would prove to be only that—background. The meat and potatoes of all this was still a little further in my future. And they'd be the craziest meat and potatoes in all the years of the history of man.

After a little while of driving, having settled in for the long trip, finishing off the pork rinds and soda pop we'd purchased at the gas station, Dad began his long story.

"Jimmy, we've got all the time in the world on our hands now, so I will try to answer a lot of the questions that must be driving you crazy. But you gotta understand there are a lot of things that I still don't know. But I'll tell you what I do know."

I put my seat back a little, excited at finally knowing what was behind everything that had happened.

"Okay, Dad, lay it on me."

He looked over at me and smiled. Driving in that car on that road in the middle of nowhere, sitting back with a pile of junk food, it almost seemed like old times. Until he started his story.

"I don't know the best way to tell it but to start at the beginning, so here goes.

"It starts with your grandpa—at least for our part in the story anyway. He worked for a man named Custer Bleak. From what you've said since we left the lake, I believe this is the man you like to call Raspy. Sounds crazy, but that's the same thing I used to call him as a kid. He's got quite the voice, doesn't he?"

I nodded, but didn't say anything.

"That's as good a name as any other, so let's stick to it. Jimmy, Raspy was an old man when I was a kid. And he still is. How to explain that, I don't know, but the guy has been ancient since my dad—your grandpa—knew him. And he's always been a crusty old geezer. He owned a factory over in Lawrenceville, and made a bundle of money—your grandpa was his accountant for a long time.

"Well, back in the '60s, old Raspy, my dad, and Borbus Duck—senior, mind you—started a group, a gentlemen's club, and called it the Union of Knights. It only had a few members, and no one really knew what their purpose was. All people knew was that they met every Thursday night, usually not until about nine o'clock. The subjects and discussions of their meetings were kept very secret. But, people didn't really care too much—they just figured they were drinking and talking about nothing.

"But they weren't talking about nothing, Jimmy. Let me just tell you that they were up to no good. Raspy gained unbelievable power over our town—he's had complete control over the police for years and years. That's why some people call him the Sheriff. It's like that Union became Duluth's very own mafia."

Dad paused for a minute, just staring ahead as the painted lines of the freeway continued to disappear one after the other under our car. It was kind of hypnotizing, with the darkness of the countryside broken up only by our headlights. We were really out in the boondocks, and there didn't appear to be another soul in sight.

Dad continued.

"Jimmy, somehow Raspy had come across what he deemed 'The Legend of the Door.' How he did—that's a part of the story that's not clear. But my dad once said that Raspy claimed it had come to him in a 'vision of shadow,' whatever the heck that means. But anyway, he was obsessed with it. He said that the Legend would lead to unbelievable power—that whoever discovered it could literally rule the world. And the Union of Knights' sole purpose was to research and discover this legend. They had tons of money and tons of time.

"Raspy was really the only one who knew anything. He got his information from somewhere, but nobody knew where. But somehow he was getting hints here and there, and through the years, the Union got closer and closer to its goal.

"Well, they found this door—right in our little town of Duluth, Georgia. Dad said that Raspy claimed that was why he had been chosen to discover the Legend—because he was closest to it. You know those woods on the west side of the neighborhood that lead out to Lake Norman and old Mrs. Jones' place?"

"Yeah," I said, "I go there all the time to climb trees. Dad, that's where I saw Mayor Duck kill that woman! Is that where the door is?"

"Yeah. You've probably never noticed it, but it looks like an old door that somebody abandoned out in the woods with a bunch of other garbage. I mean, it doesn't look like a door-way into the ground or anything like that—it just looks like an old door that somebody dropped on the forest floor."

I thought about it, and sure enough, I knew I *had* seen that old door. I had noticed it before, but never thought twice about it. I even remember thinking one time, wouldn't that be cool if there was something weird under that door? That gave me chills. I told Dad that.

"Well, it should give you chills. It's the strangest thing, Jimmy. When I was a little kid, that door was there, and it's still there today. People who see it just walk on by. You try explaining to me why in all these years no one has ever tried throwing that thing away or something. Well, now that I think about it, maybe people have. They just had no luck, and soon forgot about it."

"What're you talking about?"

"Finding the door was the first big discovery by the Union. But they were soon sorely disappointed. Jimmy, this is where the story goes from strange to beyond belief. That door could not be moved, lifted—nothing. Obviously their first instinct was to look under the thing. It was like trying to lift a hundred-year-old oak tree. Not even the slightest budge—not the slightest. And this really freaked them out because to their eyes, it literally looked like it was just a door lying on some leaves. My dad said it was the weirdest sensation to look at it and not be able to lift it.

"So they tried digging around it. They might as well have tried to dig a hole in Stone Mountain with a plastic spoon. The ground below and around it was hard stone. They tried digging far away and then tunneling toward it—no luck. They tried dynamite. Nothing. It was like someone had put a magical stone shield around and under that blasted Door.

"After weeks of useless attempts, they gave up, and returned to their research."

I asked Dad what he meant when he said they researched.

"Well, they looked in every book you can imagine—from ancient Native American myths to archived tabloids about aliens and monsters from other worlds. When I say research, I say they looked at any and every thing they could think of that might mention some kind of legend about a door.

"But it was always Raspy who came up with new discoveries. The next big one was that to open the Door, you needed a special key, and that there was a book that told where the key was. You believing all this, Jimmy?"

I looked over at him, and kind of shrugged my shoulders.

"I guess. A few days ago I would've said you were a crazy old fool teasing his son, but after what I've seen recently, I guess I do believe you."

"Well, son, I am *not* teasing you. You've got to believe every word I say, because if we're going to get our family

JAMES DASHNER ✧ 71

out of this mess, I need your help in figuring out what to do. And in order for you to do that, you've gotta know the background."

"Dad, I promise I'll believe you—you've never lied to me before."

"Good. Like I said, somehow Raspy found out that there was a book about this Legend, and in it was the location of a *key* to open that stupid Door. And that's where I come in."

"What do ya mean?" I asked.

"Raspy said the book was in Japan of all places, and that he wanted me to go and find it. That's when things went sour for your grandpa. He told Raspy there was no chance that I was going to get involved in this thing—I had a wife and a couple of kids, you included, Jimmy. But Raspy persisted that I was the logical choice, because I had studied Japanese in college.

"Well, your grandpa flat-out refused. And then he was murdered, Jimmy. By Raspy's men."

The inside of the car fell silent for several minutes.

✦CHAPTER 16✦

The Enemy

I couldn't believe what I was hearing. Dad had always said Grandpa died in a volcano. Now that I think about it, what kind of dumb kid would believe that story? I never knew Grandpa, so knowing he was killed was shocking, but it wasn't as nearly heart-wrenching to me as it obviously was to Dad.

"Raspy came to see me one day to tell me how 'sorry' he was that my dad had to meet such a terrible ending. And then he kindly said that if I didn't want the same to happen to my kids and wife, that I'd be taking a trip to Japan. You're too young to remember, Jimmy, but I had no choice, and I went to Japan. Can you believe that? I went to Japan for some old crusty murderer to find his magical book about a key!"

Dad got emotional, and I thought for sure the old bear was going to cry.

Japan. That surely would be the last place I would've expected to enter into this story. Why would the book talking about a Door in Georgia be clear over in Japan? Dad continued.

"Raspy told me that if I came back without the book, he'd kill one of my kids. Jimmy, that man was getting more and more evil. He was obsessed, and he had lost all sense of reality. And he had the means to do what he promised. So I went. And I was there a long time."

Old Joseph popped in my head right then, and I suddenly understood.

The photo album.

"Dad! How long were you gone? Did Joseph take care of us?"

"Well . . . yes. Yeah, he did. How in the world did you know that?"

"Joseph showed me a photo album with a bunch of pictures of him and our family to show me that I could trust him. But after a while I realized that you weren't in any of those pictures—not one of 'em!"

"Crazy Joseph. He was always kind of a weird one, but I could trust him. Not knowing how long I'd be gone, I asked him to stay with my family until I got back. Who knew it would take a year."

I was stunned.

"A year!?"

"Longest year of my life. I lived in that country for one whole year. I looked everywhere from Sapporo in the north to Nagasaki in the south. That was one crazy year, Jimmy, and some day I'll tell you more about it. But let me just tell you one thing—this world is not what you think it is. And I don't think that door or that book or the key are even from this world at all, at least not what we think of as our world. Japan changed me, and scared me, and made me realize that the last thing on the earth we wanted was for the key to the door to get in the hands of Raspy. This legend business is for real, and if Raspy . . . discovers whatever it is, our little lives are in for a change for the worse."

I grew more and more excited—and scared—about the whole story.

"So, what happened there? Did you find the book? The key? What happened?"

"To make a long story short, I found the book. It took

some major effort, and a few scary nights along the way, but I found it. The key was also in Japan, and that just about killed me getting that thing. But I did, and I made it back. With the key, but not the book—I left that there, right where I found it."

"Why'd you leave the book there?"

"It said right on the first page that if it was taken out of that ... place, that it would burn right up, taking whoever happened to be holding the thing right then with it. After what I'd seen that year, I wasn't going to take any chances on that.

"I brought the key back to Georgia. I didn't know what to do, because I was so scared to give it to Raspy. But I knew if I didn't, he'd kill my family for sure. So in the end, I just gave it to him, and hoped that somehow he could be stopped. It was a stupid decision by a desperate and terrified man. But it turned out okay.

"Raspy had no patience. The very night after I got home, he made us all go with him to visit the door. He was so strange that day, laughing at nothing, mumbling to himself—it was very disturbing.

"There was no moon that night—it was very, very dark. And I felt scared to death. It was just Raspy, Borbus Duck Sr., his son the mayor, and me that night. I guess Raspy wanted me to be with him in case the key didn't work and he needed someone to take out his anger on. When we got to the door, the whole woods seemed to go dead silent. It was downright creepy. And Raspy made his way to open the thing, and to find his precious legend—whatever it may be.

"But it wasn't going to happen. Out of the woods, we were suddenly attacked by a bunch of men wearing masks. We had no chance—they took the key and were gone as quickly as they had come. Raspy went into a rage.

"It wasn't until years later that I found out that the whole thing had been planned by Joseph. I had told him all about my fears, and he took matters into his own hands. I guess he called a bunch of his whacked-out cousins, and they did the job for him. Joseph never told me because he didn't want to take any chances of Raspy finding out that I was involved. Although he's suspected it ever since.

"That was nine years ago, Jimmy, and things have quieted down since then—until right before your little incident. The only reason I've been alive all these years, and y'all included, is because Raspy knew if he had us killed that he would certainly never see the key again. I was his only thread of hope. And he suspected that Joseph knew where the key was located, and thought he'd get back to me eventually. So he's been watching us like a hawk—even intercepting and reading our mail. I found this out right after I sent you to Utah.

"Raspy came to my house and said he knew everything— that Joseph had the key, that he was in Utah, and that I had sent you there. Joseph had just sent me a letter, so I knew that was how Raspy must've found out about everything. Before that, I had not heard from Joseph in seven or eight years. In the letter, he had given me his phone number, address, everything. That was why I sent you there. And when I found out Raspy had read the letter, I knew you were in a heap of trouble. I knew he'd send somebody.

"So, I did something crazy. I told Raspy that Joseph called me and told me where he had hidden the key, and that I would go get it. It was stupid, but I was trying to buy time. I begged him to give me this one shot to make everything okay—to not do anything crazy to my family or to you. I told him to give me twenty-four hours. He agreed.

"I immediately put your mom and Rusty on the Amtrak, and sent them to Washington, D.C. I told them to then go straight to the airport and buy two tickets to Omaha,

Nebraska, and to go stay at the Best Western Hotel down-town. I said to stay there until we come meet them. Jimmy, I hope on my life that they are there. Oh, please be there."

Dad paused for a long time.

"Anyway, then I took the first flight out here. It was a stupid risk to take, 'cause I was just sure Raspy would have people following me. But I had no choice—I knew he would send someone to get you, and I had to try and come. Now, I'm just worried sick that I've jeopardized Rusty and your mom's life to save yours. Oh, Jimmy, what if they're not there? I can't stand it."

I was in a daze. The jumbled story my dad had just thrown out cleared up a few things, but it was still just nuts. I didn't even know what questions to ask.

"Dad, how did you find me in the middle of that lake?"

A look came over his face. A shadow of fear. He didn't say a word.

"Dad?"

He stayed silent.

"Dad? How did you find me?"

"Jimmy, the story ain't quite finished. I haven't really told you the . . . most frightening part about all this."

I waited. Dad suddenly looked different.

"Raspy, Mayor Duck, the others, they're not just—. They're not just bad people. I think they, uh, well." He just kind of looked at me with a strange smile on his face.

"You think what?" I asked.

"I think they're not . . . human . . . anymore."

"Not human?" *Could this get any weirder?*

"I mean, they're human, but . . . I think they're being controlled, or something. I can't explain it. But the point is, they leave a trace of something wherever they go. Somehow I've learned how to look for it. Ya know that blackness that we saw at the lake?"

"Yeah."

"It's kind of like that. A ... darkness, a darkness that I've learned how to sense. I literally drove around Salt Lake until I could sense it, and that's how I found out where you guys had stayed in a hotel. When I got there, you guys had checked out a couple of hours before—I asked the people at the desk about a little boy with a hairy guy named Dontae."

"You knew Hairy?"

"Yes, Jimmy—he's one of the Union. And Raspy took great pleasure in telling me who he sent to get you. When I say he took pleasure in telling me, it's because he knows that of all of them, Dontae, or Hairy, is the one I fear the most. Anyway, I could still sense the darkness in the air, and I followed the direction in which it seemed to grow stronger. It was obvious that you guys had gotten on the freeway and headed south. So I followed, driving like it was the Indy 500. And then I could almost see the darkness over that lake—it was the closest it had ever come to actually being visible. I know this sounds crazy—but maybe not so crazy after what we just saw. That blackness, maybe that's the same thing somehow. I don't know.

"Anyway, I ran to the docks and rented a wave runner, the best they had, and I took off. You know the rest."

The darkness outside seemed to be pushing in on our little car, like the stuff my dad described was all around us, and that we'd never escape. I started to feel scared and hopeless. *What could all this possibly mean*, I wondered. A book, a key to a mystical door, a Union of strange people with images of darkness appearing around them, swallowing boats like a saber-toothed tiger in the tar pits—only a lot quicker. A Legend of great power—through a door that had never been opened. I was starting to get a little creeped out.

I wished it was light outside. After a while of dreadful thoughts, Dad spoke again.

"Well, son, there's probably still more I could tell you, but I'm sick of talking right now. We should be in Omaha in a couple of hours."

"Okay. Dad?"

"Yeah, son."

"What do you think these people are? Aliens? Devils?"

"I don't know Jimmy, but be very afraid of them. I remember a line in that book in Japan. It was kind of an eerie statement. And I'm sure it has a lot to do with the evil intentions behind the Union."

"What did it say?"

Dad paused, then took a long breath.

"It said, 'Be brave. The Stompers are coming.'"

✧CHAPTER 17✧

Geezer

Salt Lake City, and then Omaha, Nebraska. Never in my life did I ever think I'd someday go to those places or anywhere else west of the Mississippi. For all I knew, that was another country.

Later I would look back at those thoughts and laugh. My list of strange places visited would soon make Utah and Nebraska seem as ordinary as going to the bathroom.

It was just past dawn when we rolled into town in that rental car. I had fallen asleep and woke up when I sensed the car slowing to get off the freeway. I began to get that nervous knot in my stomach wondering if my family would be there. As I rubbed my eyes and woke up, I fell back into that bucket of fear I'd started to grow accustomed to. Who knew what we would find—maybe Raspy and his dogs would be there waiting for us.

My dad pulled into a gas station and looked through the pages of a phone book. He ran back to the car and jumped in.

"There are two Best Westerns in town. Let's go."

They were not at the first one. We panicked a little, but knew there was still one more to check.

They were not at the second one.

But they had been.

The lady at the desk told us that two people had checked in under the name Fincher just a couple of days ago. But they up and left in a hurry without even checking out late the night before. She said they left with two men. Our stomachs turned over at hearing that.

As we were talking to the lady at the hotel, I noticed an old man sitting in a chair in the front lobby, just staring at me like I was a leper or something. He didn't look too happy to see me. I tried to ignore him, but it kept bothering me.

Dad explained to the lady that he was Mrs. Fincher's husband and asked if he could go look at the room. She checked his driver's license and figured there weren't many Finchers in the world, so she took us up.

It was your typical hotel room. Two queen-sized beds, a tiny TV, a little round table with a lamp on it. There were a couple of paintings that looked like a first grader spilled some watercolors and called it good. The beds were not made. A couple of open suitcases sat on the floor over by the table. We looked in the bathroom, and Mom's stuff was in there, laid out all over the sink counter.

They definitely had *not* been planning on leaving.

Dad didn't know what to do, and neither did I.

We gathered their stuff and went out and put it in the car. Dad paid the lady for the hotel room, and left her his cell phone number in case they came back.

But my dad and I both knew one thing—they weren't coming back to this hotel. There was no doubt in either of our minds that Raspy now had my mom and brother. We could barely walk we were so distressed.

As we walked back out to the car, the old man appeared again. He was leaning against the brick wall of the hotel, facing our car. I nudged Dad and whispered to him to take a look at the old, scary-looking guy. Dad shrugged, and put his key in the car door to open it.

Then the geezer spoke. He had a scraggly, worn-out voice, like he'd talked his vocal chords out of business years ago.

"You folks looking for a woman and her boy?"

Dad snapped to attention, and frantically ran over to the man.

"Yes, yes! We're looking for my wife and son. What do you know?"

"Know? I don't know nothing! All I can say is what I saw. Nothing else."

He gave a scowl in my direction, and I wondered what I'd ever done to this old cuss of a man.

"Okay, sir, fine—what did you see?" my dad asked, anxious and impatient.

"Swallowed up, I tell ya. Like Jonah and the whale. Burn my pants, swallowed 'em right up. Never seen nothing like it, I tell ya." Geezer spit a nice juicy one over to the side, wiped his chin, and looked back at me with a scowl.

"Sir, what do you mean? What swallowed up who?"

Geezer suddenly looked scared, like he'd just woken up beside an alligator.

"I don't know, I tell ya. Maybe I shouldn't be talking to you no-how. Leave me be!"

He started to move away. My dad wasn't going to let that happen.

He grabbed Geezer's arm, and turned him around, gently.

"Look, old man, we're the last people on earth who would ever hurt you. Please, we are desperately trying to find my wife and kid—we think they've been taken by some very bad people. Please help us with anything—anything you've got or know. Please!"

Geezer shook with fright and let out a little whimper.

"Please don't hurt me. Please. I didn't mean to see it—I didn't!"

"What?" my dad yelled. Beyond impatient, he was getting downright livid.

"The Shadow! The Shadow! The Shadow! I saw it—it swallowed them whole! Please, leave me be!"

He jerked his arm away—only because my dad let him. Geezer stumbled away, mumbling something about Jonah and the whale. It was obviously useless to try to get anything out of this guy. Plus, we both started having a feeling that we knew what the old man was talking about.

My dad looked at me, and said that we would get nothing more from the old man. Dad motioned to the car and we got in. He started it up, but then sunk back in the seat and took a deep breath.

"Jimmy, this shadow he's talking about. It must be the same thing as the lake. It must be. What have I done? How could I have left them?"

My dad broke into tears, his body shaking as he sobbed and groaned.

"What have I done?" he mumbled beneath his sobs.

I didn't know what to say or do. I felt like I was in some kind of dream.

What was that Blackness that had swallowed the boat? And what was this Blackness that supposedly had also swallowed Mom and Rusty?

What is it?

Dad stopped crying after a few minutes, and wiped his eyes and face. He then looked over at me, and tried his hardest to smile. He failed miserably.

"Jimmy, I know they're not dead. I don't know what this Shadow, Blackness business is, but I can't help but think it's not the end of life when you enter it. Otherwise, why would Dontae—Hairy—have been heading straight for it in that boat?"

"Yeah, Dad, you're right." I said, feeling like I sounded stupid and hollow. But he had made a great point. Maybe it was . . . I couldn't even come up with one guess.

"That door," Dad said, "That dang door and its stupid legend. That's gotta be our only hope."

Dad put the car into reverse and slammed on the gas, making the tires screech so bad it about gave me a heart attack.

He slapped me on the leg, put the car into drive, and sped off toward the freeway.

"We're going back to Georgia, Jimmy."

✦CHAPTER 18✦

Looking for a Tree

I told my dad everything about my adventures as well during the long road trip. He finally had to pull over at a rest stop and sleep for a few hours—I'd never seen a person so exhausted in my life. The trip took another day or so from Omaha, and finally, we were heading into familiar country. The skyline of Atlanta loomed on the horizon when we started really planning what we were going to do. We had no choice but to try and follow Joseph's clues and find the key.

"Okay, Jimmy," Dad said, "You told me 'Old Willow's Trunk.' Now, I can think of two big willow trees that have been around for ages, and both of them were very familiar to Joseph. One is down by the Chattahoochee River in the park where Joseph and I used to take you kids. It was famous for being so old, but I never remember anybody ever calling it 'Old Willow.' Also, there's one by Joseph's old house that has a big tire swing on it. Knowing Joseph, he probably did name trees, like some crazy person."

I tried my hardest to grin and nod like I agreed with him how crazy that would be.

"I reckon Joseph could've bored a hole into the trunk or something and hid the key, then put the drilled part back into it. That would be very hard to find, and the odds of Raspy ever even looking for it there would be pretty much zero. Let's go check those out first."

"But what about Mom and Rusty?" I said, having assumed

the first thing we'd do is somehow save our family.

"Jimmy, I just don't know what we can do. If we find that key, maybe that will either lead us to something that will help, or if worse comes to worse, we'll trade Raspy the darn thing for our family. I just don't know what we can do right now to those monsters. So let's at least do something for now. If it doesn't lead to anything good, we'll try something else. Okay?"

I nodded, but just felt sick inside not doing anything right away to get Mom and Rusty back. So, we went to the park to look for Old Willow. And then we went to the woods behind Joseph's old house.

Nothing.

We searched and searched those two trees, ripping off bark, climbing up into the branches, digging into the surrounding ground. Nothing, nothing, nothing.

We even looked around for other willow trees, and still found nothing.

We searched all day.

Dad, finally about to collapse with fatigue, gave up, and we went in and checked into a hotel for the night. No way we could chance going back to the house.

As I struggled to fall asleep that night, thoughts of Joseph's last words kept going through my head over and over. We were missing something. But he hadn't given us too much material to work with.

Old Willow's Trunk.

Tomorrow we'll find that stupid tree and that stupid key, I thought, trying to stay positive as I finally started to fall asleep.

In one of those quirks of life, I'd end up being both wrong and right at the same time.

✧ ✧ ✧

The next day, we were back at it.

Dad said that the grounds in front of city hall had a bunch of trees, and that some of them were willows. So we tried there, and looked around all morning. Still, nothing.

We were sitting on a bench, resting, eating a couple of sandwiches that my dad had bought at a little store next to city hall, when once again, things turned topsy-turvy and inside out.

I was in the middle of a bite, just about to mention that maybe we'd better not just sit in the open like this, when Dad dropped his sandwich and stood up, pulling me up with him. His grip on my arm hurt, and I knew trouble had come.

"Jimmy, they're here."

The way he said it was so strange. I was learning more and more about the odd ways humans react in awful situations. He didn't scream, he didn't go nuts, he just calmly said that we had company, that 'they' were here. I looked where he was looking.

Across the great big lawn in front of the city buildings, running full speed, straight toward us, were the last two people I cared to see right then.

Hairy and Monster.

My first thought was that Hairy was not dead, and had obviously gotten back to Georgia pretty darn quick.

My second thought was that we'd better get the heck out of there.

Dad grabbed my shoulder, and we started running.

My heart bursting, my breath exploding, I ran as hard as I could. We headed for the group of buildings by the city hall.

The thugs weren't too close, and I thought we could easily lose them once we got out of that big open space. We almost made it.

But then I heard the shot, and then I sensed more than saw my dad go down. I turned around in shock, and saw my dad lying on the ground, holding his leg. I was horrified.

"Jimmy," he screamed, "it's just my leg! You go! Go!"

"Dad," I pleaded, "Come on, I'll help you!"

"Son, you go, you go now! We've got no choice! GO!"

My mind spun in a million directions. My heart was ripped apart. The pain of seeing my own dad hurt by those gutless freaks overwhelmed me. But my dad was right, and I did the hardest thing I'd ever done.

I went.

✧CHAPTER 19✧

Old Willow

The panic was killing me. The whole shabang of the last few days, culminating in seeing my dad get shot and taken by those thugs, churned inside my gut and made me want to puke. Not to mention there were people out there who sure seemed to want me dead as soon as they could manage it.

I looked out from behind the trash thingy I was hiding behind, close to the city buildings, and it sure looked like there was no one around. *They must've given up and went away*, I thought. I hoped.

I knew I had to get away from there before they came back. I took a chance and darted right across the front lawn of the city building, hoping to catch a bus that looked to be stopping right that minute. I'd been running for about 4 seconds when something to my left caught the corner of my eye like a rusty fishhook on a catfish. At the time I didn't even know what it was, but it stopped me dead in my tracks.

I slowly looked over to my left. It was under a nice shady tree, and there was a bench right next to it. Something about it brought a surge of memories into my little noggin—a whole bunch of jumbled memories that didn't quite make any sense yet.

The object holding the attention of my beady eyes was a statue. I must have seen it a hundred times before, never really even noticing it. Until now.

It was a statue of an elephant.

I walked, then ran straight toward it. My thoughts started churning, and I remembered a bedtime story from my mom. Something about a famous elephant, and how he had come to Duluth with the circus, and had gotten sick, making the ringmaster ask if he could leave the animal here for our people to take care of, and how he had kind of become an icon or something to our little town, and how his name had been . . .

I almost fell down dead before I got there. I didn't even need to look at the commemorative plaque.

Old Willow. The elephant's name had been Old Willow.

✧ ✧ ✧

He stared at me like I was some kind of peanut ready for him to eat. Thank goodness he wasn't a life-sized statue, or I guess I'd have had to go and buy a ladder. It was just a little miniature thing, with a plaque telling his story. Right then and there I didn't give a flip what his story was, because I finally knew what the heck old Joseph had been blabbering about when he dropped dead right in front of me.

The key.

Old Willow's trunk hung down from his head like a fat, dead snake, and almost touched the ground. I put my hands on it and started to feel around. I just about wet my pants when I realized that the thing was hollow. You could just tell.

I looked around behind me to see if anyone was looking. Like anyone gave a hoot about some kid looking at a statue of an elephant. I looked back at Old Willow. Did I dare?

Sure enough I did.

I stepped back, and pretending I was a kung fu expert now, I kicked that poor elephant's trunk as hard as my skinny foot could kick. Then I realized 'poor elephant' nothing—I thought my leg was a goner. I fell down it hurt so bad.

It reminded me of how it feels when you're not quite holding the baseball bat tight enough when you hit the ball.

I looked at Old Willow's trunk in desperation.

There was a crack.

Excited, I forgot my hurt leg and I kicked again. Bigger crack.

The third kick did the trick.

I yanked up the trunk piece that fell on the ground, turned it upside down and started shaking it like crazy. Something fell out onto the ground.

It was a piece of velvet, or a velvet bag, or something. I picked it up, and sure enough, it was a bag. I opened it. I looked inside it.

A key.

I took it out. It looked like one of those old-fashioned keys from storybooks—a circular ring as a handle, extending into a thick line of metal with various odds and ends sticking out on one side. I just couldn't believe it. All that time wasted looking for a dang willow tree. I stared in wonder at the tarnished metal.

The Key.

The Door.

The Legend.

It was time to get moving.

✧CHAPTER 20✧

Into the Forest

I couldn't believe it. I had seen that old nasty door lying on the ground a million times in my short little life. It lay near the same trail that led back to Ol' Betsy—the tree that started this whole mess. And as I thought about it on the way there, I couldn't believe that I'd never taken a peek at it before. I was the exploring-est kid you ever saw, and I was mad at myself for not at least looking at the dang thing. Of course, then maybe I would have met the same fate as that poor woman Mayor Duck killed.

I had no doubts that there are things in this world that we just could have never dreamed in a million years. I figured there must be something magical guarding the door, or surely somebody would've tried to throw the thing out by now. Maybe it just made people forget about it, or maybe not even see it! I was starting to think like I was in a science fiction book or something. And then I had the strange thought that maybe I was. Things were getting weirder by the day.

I knew there was a big chance Raspy might be waiting for me there. But there was nothing else to do. They had my dad, I couldn't go to the police, I had no idea where the rest of my family was, and I was plumb out of ideas. My only thought was to go to that dang door and find out what all the fuss was about. I figured they didn't know I had the key, so maybe they wouldn't think I'd go to The Door. For that matter, I wasn't so sure they even knew that I knew where

The Door was located. But they had my dad, and who knew what they'd made him tell them.

I finally got frustrated with all those jumbled thoughts and threw them right out of my head. I was going, and that was that.

✧ ✧ ✧

It took me forever and a day, but I finally got to the woods. I decided to go to the entrance behind Mrs. Jones' place, instead of the one on the other side near my house. I didn't want to go anywhere near my house, because I thought that would be way too easy a way for me to get caught by those monsters.

It grew dark by the time I got there.

Mrs. Jones lived in an old, old house, and she lived all by herself. I know I joked about how fat the woman was, but really, she's a nice lady. She's never said one mean word to me in all my life. And I can't say that for a lot of old folks. Seems like most of them just assume we youngsters are nothing but troublemakers.

Her house sat back in the woods, and the trail started right behind her shed where she kept all of her garden stuff. I was hoping she wouldn't be around because I didn't feel like explaining to her that I was on my way to find out about a magical door that hopefully led to some treasure or power that I could use to save my family from evil bad guys.

She was nowhere to be seen, and soon I was on the trail. By the time I got there, it had already grown pretty dark outside. I felt relived I had the flashlight in my backpack.

There's something awfully creepy about the woods at night. The thick, tall pine trees towered above me, and I felt like I was in a tunnel. I looked up and couldn't see a thing but branches and leaves. No stars, no moon. When I shone the flashlight ahead of me, it was like it could only go so far—it seemed like it hit a wall of blackness about twenty feet ahead. The trail below my feet was covered with leaves and twigs, and every step made a soft crunching sound that felt mighty ominous in the strange, dark quiet that hung over me. There was the sound of insects and such, but you didn't really hear them unless you stopped and thought about it.

I kept moving. I knew exactly where to find The Door, and I was getting anxious.

✧CHAPTER 21✧

A Door in the Woods

Before long, I arrived. Ol' Betsy loomed over me, and a rush of nightmares of that first day came back and hit me like the blunt end of an axe. I guess the fear had subsided throughout my long walk a little bit, but it returned in full force as I sat and gazed up at Ol' Betsy. I wondered if I would ever climb that tree again.

I moved on about another fifty feet or so, and there it was.

The Door.

The Legend.

And for all I could tell there wasn't another soul around. No Raspy, no Hairy, no Monster, no hairy monsters.

Could it all really be true? Was there really something below that old rotted door? There had to be. But I worried I would pick it up and see a bunch of Georgia red mud and centipedes. If the thing didn't crumble when I lifted it.

For a minute, I sat there and stared.

It was a big door, the darkest, deepest brown I'd ever seen, and it looked like it had lain there for a hundred years. The color of the wood looked natural—like it had never been painted, or else the paint had faded away years before. The closer I looked, the more I realized that it wasn't just your run-of-the-mill door that came off the front of your neighbor's house. It seemed . . . curvy, with no hard edges. The overall shape was definitely rectangular, but there was something really odd about its edges. There were carvings along the face of it—but they were too worn down to tell what they were. And there were no panels on it or anything. It was just a big, weird-looking piece of wood.

With no handle.

Dad's story about all the things the Union had done to try and open it had been beyond belief to me. How could a bunch of men not just open the thing? Pick it up and heave it over? Dad had said that even dynamite didn't work. It didn't make any sense.

I crept closer, the sudden sound of the leaves under my feet scaring me half to death. I put my fingers under the edges, and lifted. Or, *tried* to lift, I should say.

Nothing.

It was like trying to lift a house. Not even the slightest budge.

I tried again on the other side and then on the shorter sides.

Nothing.

I kicked it, and it felt like kicking stone. I tried digging some dirt from around its edges and soon found solid rock. I tried here and there, sinking my fingers into the dirt, trying to dig something. That door was completely surrounded by pure stone. My excitement built right along with my frustration. I finally started to believe my dad about how this door just didn't want to open. So . . . the key.

I took it out of my backpack, looked at its strange shape and tarnished metal, and knelt back down to find myself a keyhole.

I searched and searched with my flashlight, up and down, along the edges—I couldn't see anything even close to a hole. I got so frustrated I wanted to climb Ol' Betsy and scream. Why was this so difficult? Who ever heard of a door with no handle or keyhole, or *something*!

I started thinking about my dad. He'd kept trying to convince me that the world was no longer quite what I thought it was, and sometimes things aren't what they seem.

I decided to sit down and think about it. I plopped down and stared at the . . .

There it was. An old, gnarled tree stood about three feet away from The Door. And two feet up from the ground, snuggled between some twisted bark on the tree, there was a metal plate, old and rusted. In the middle of that plate was a keyhole.

I just about pulled a muscle jumping up and running over to that tree. There it was, a keyhole! I wondered if anyone had ever noticed it before—it was so difficult to see because of the twisted, gnarled bark around it.

I kneeled down before it, took the key, and pushed it into the hole. It slid in as smooth as putting a spoon in a bowl of cereal. I turned it to the right and heard a click. For some reason, I hadn't expected a click—I thought angels would come down from heaven or something, but all it did was click.

Ever since that day I first saw the Mayor up to his murdering ways, my sense of normal and rational thought had begun to fade. Every day, it seemed, I had a new lesson in how the world didn't work the way I thought it did. Well, when I turned around to look at the door, anything left in my mind having to do with "normal" officially departed.

The Door had vanished. Not opened—vanished.

Where it had been was a big hole. The Door hadn't moved—it was just plain gone. I crawled over to the hole. I shone the flashlight down and let out a little gasp of excitement.

Below me, a set of dark, damp, gray stone stairs descended into the hole, starting from where I knelt and curving down into the earth like a spiral, with no railing. Even with my flashlight, I couldn't see it end—it looked for all the world like a spiral staircase to China.

I felt scared a little but even more excited. Without much of a thought, I picked up my backpack, threw it over my shoulders, and started down the stone stairwell.

I had found The Key, I had opened The Door.

Now for The Legend.

✧CHAPTER 22✧

The Hole

I hugged the wall as I began my journey down the hole. When I hit the eighth step, I heard a quick humming sound that was gone as soon as it had come. Something felt . . . different. I looked up, and yelled out in fright.

The Door was back, and I was now on the inside.

I ran back up the few stairs and soon heard the humming sound again. The Door disappeared, this time with me looking at it. It was like a cheap video game or something—one second it was there, the next it wasn't. No cool fade or explosion into mist or anything. I could again see the spooky shapes of tree branches and leaves through the opening.

I resumed my descent into the darkness below.

Soon the humming, and The Door was back. I figured that's the way this place worked, and I kept going.

The air felt very damp, and it was cold. It seemed strange since it was the middle of summer, but I felt like I had one of those misting machines they have at the Braves stadium for really hot days. I was sure my hair and clothes would be soaked before too long.

And the darkness. Even with my flashlight, it felt like a blanket. And there was not a sound to be heard but the light, muffled taps my feet made on the stone stairs.

I kept going—slowly, and carefully—but I kept going.

I decided to count the stairs.

Ten, twenty, thirty.

Nothing changed as I went deeper. Every step brought another one that looked just like it. The damp stone walls were smooth as if they had been worn by waves from the ocean for a million years. Which also made me realize that this whole . . . cave or whatever must have been carved, because there was no sign at all of blocks or mortar or anything. The walls and the stairs were made of continuous stone. Stone dark with wetness.

When I hit fifty steps, I stopped. I couldn't believe that this thing just kept going! In fact, there was nothing about anything that made sense. But I had grown accustomed to that.

I started again, and at seventy-two, I hit the bottom.

The curving stairwell became a long passage—a tunnel of stone that led in a straight line from where I was standing for as far as I could see.

And, I noticed, the weirdness was only beginning.

Set in the walls of the tunnel, one about every twenty feet or so, were burning torches.

Burning torches. Two hours before I would have thought that impossible.

Now, having light provided by impossible torches, I put my flashlight back into my pack.

I walked straight ahead. I swear I went a mile. It kept going and going, the torches regular in their intervals along the walls, and the stone looking the same the whole way— dark, gray, and wet. The tunnel finally ended at another wooden door, one that looked just like The Door I had opened up in the woods. Except this one had a handle—a big, curved piece of iron, with both ends attached to the wood. I grabbed it and pulled. It opened pretty easily, without the creak I would've expected in such a spooky place.

Thoughts of what I had been through had gone through my head the whole time I walked through that long, torch-lit passage. A group called the Union of Knights. A man named Joseph who dressed like a cartoon and was my daddy for a year. A key inside the trunk of an elephant. A door that vanishes, and freshly lit torches where supposedly there was no one to light them. All strange, and all beyond belief. But nothing could have prepared me for what was in that room.

I walked inside.

It was a small cavern, with similar torches hanging on the walls and the same damp, smooth stone walls and floor. In the middle of the room sat a huge iron chair, with massive arms, legs and back. All kinds of eerie carvings were on the chair, carvings of animals and strange creatures, and things that looked like . . . boats or something. It was surely the craziest, ugliest chair I had ever seen. But that was nothing.

Sitting on the chair, with hands folded, and eyes boring into mine, was a young girl.

A *living*, young girl.

She had long, long hair, and it was as brown as the wooden door. She was dressed in a T-shirt and jeans. And sneakers.

I could not breathe.

She tilted her head, gave me a smile—one of sadness, not joy—and, with a voice that sounded like flutes playing inside a cathedral, spoke.

"It's about time, Jimmy Fincher."

For the first time in my life, in a stone room in the middle of the earth, I fainted.

✧CHAPTER 23✧

Farmer

Eventually, I woke up.

I was lying on my back in the same room as before. Still kind of dazed, I sat up and looked around. The iron chair was still there, but instead of the little girl, now sitting there was an old, old man. He was dressed like a farmer, with dirty, torn jeans and a flannel shirt that looked like it'd been worn during a few harvests without being washed. What hair he had left was white, and his face sported a scraggly beard. I was shocked once again by the latest development in my little adventure, but the scary thing was that I was only shocked a little. I was actually starting to get used to it.

I couldn't think of one word to say. I just stared.

Almost in a whisper, he spoke after a few seconds.

"Like we said, Jimmy, it's about time."

I stared some more. He stared right back, with not the least hint of a smile. So I decided I better say something.

"Like *we* said? What're you talking about? Where's that girl?"

"She is onto other business, Jimmy. However, she is me and I am she. We are one."

I kind of spun my legs around and sat cross-legged, facing the old man. I was sick of being confused, and asking questions that just made it worse. I was also getting braver and braver in my discussions with strange people.

"Look, mister, can't you tell that I don't have the slightest clue what's going on here? I'm a fourteen-year-old boy who a few days ago didn't do anything but go to school, climb trees, and watch baseball. Your talk about you being a she is all fine and dandy, but would you please take just one minute and tell me what the heck is going on? Where am I? Who are you? How come you live in the ground?"

Not the most brilliant questions in the world, but I sure hoped it was a start.

He gave a soft chuckle, and leaned forward, putting his elbows on his knees.

"Jimmy, to answer your first and last question, we are not in the ground, at least not in the ground where you think we would be. When you walked through the Door, you left what you understand as your world, and came to what I understand as my world. It is not something you can or ever will comprehend. At least not for a very long time."

Boy, oh boy, he was just clearing things up by the minute. He continued.

"As for who I am, well, I am whatever I want to be, in terms of how you see me. I can appear as a rock, an old man, or a roaring lion for that matter. But I know your question is much deeper than that. And again, it is a hard thing for you to comprehend.

"We are the Givers.

"But, more than anything, I am a mere messenger for now. To give *you* a message. Why you, I do not know, but out of the billions of people who have lived in your world, you alone have made it here to receive the Four Gifts. And I am only here to give you the First, tell you how to use it, and then how to obtain the Second. Once I am done, I will leave. It's that simple."

Very simple, I thought. He continued.

"What you have been searching for, this 'Legend of the Door'—well, as you know, our plan almost failed miserably.

We wanted it to be a test, to not be easy, so that we could know that the person who solved it and made it to us would be of strong character and mind. But the Shadow Ka almost took our plan and spit it right back in our faces. We've been 'rooting' for you, Jimmy, as you say in your world, but you just about didn't make it, it seems."

I was sure that I was in a mental institution, and that I was doomed for the rest of my life to have hallucinations. I couldn't talk. I just . . . I was more confused and scared than I'd ever been before. So I just sat there.

The old man leaned back in the chair, and continued once again.

"Jimmy, all you need to know is that my people have left something for you, to give hope to your world. Bad things are coming. And there is little that we can do, at least in your world—except to leave you with the Four Gifts. In the end, they could be your last hope."

Finally, I did speak.

"Old man, please, what are you talking about? I'm the last hope? Four Gifts? What are you talking about?"

"Jimmy, we would hope that a child as yourself would not be so cynical. We hoped that you would be innocent from the ways of the world. Please tell me that you are willing to believe what I am telling you."

Something told me to shut up and take his words to heart. I'd just seen a magic door and a stone staircase in the middle of the woods. Maybe things were possible that didn't seem possible. I mean, no one could've pulled this kind of joke on me, could they? Maybe our little world we like to call Earth really was in for some kind of trouble. I decided to be a little nicer to the Farmer.

"Sir, I promise you that with all my heart I will at least try to believe what you are telling me."

"That is good, Jimmy. Thank you. Look into my hand."

His right hand was sticking out and he held a golden cup of some sort. It was very smooth, and rounded, and not very big. It looked like a . . . teacup without a handle, made out of pure, shiny gold. It was filled with a shiny white liquid. I looked from the cup back into Farmer's eyes.

"This is the First Gift, Jimmy. Drink this liquid."

My mouth twitched.

"I just gave a little here," I said, irritated, "telling you that I was willing to listen. Ten seconds later you're asking me to drink something that I have no idea what it even is?"

"Jimmy, I told you what it is—it's the First Gift, the first of four. It is called The Shield. It is the First Gift, because it will help you most in obtaining the other Three. You have no idea what a powerful Gift this is, my boy."

Something inside of me felt good. A complete stranger was probably about to feed me poison, but I felt good. I had no choice. This is why I'd come here. Even more than jumping from that tree to escape Mayor Duck, I once again did the craziest thing I'd ever done, which seemed to keep happening over and over again. I took the cup and drank the liquid.

It tasted like water. It felt like water. That was it.

"So, what now? Do I die from the poison?" I asked Farmer.

"Jimmy, raise your right arm." I did.

"Now, raise your other arm." Again, I did what he said.

"Did you, in your mind, have to tell your arms to do that? Did you even have to think about it at all?"

"No, sir."

"It's as if your arm has its own brains, isn't it? You don't really think in your head, 'okay, arm, you shall now raise up in the air' do you? You just want to raise your arm, so it does—almost instantaneously, correct?"

"Yeah, I guess. What're you getting at?"

"You now have the same power with something far *more* powerful. The Shield."

"The Shield?" I asked.

Farmer reached into one of his pants pockets, and took out a rock—about the size of his fist.

"Jimmy, your entire training on how to use The Shield will take ten seconds. I will now throw this rock at you. Just like raising your arm without even thinking about it, you will then deflect it. The Shield is not something you . . . use, exactly. It is connected with your brain just like an arm, and it will be a reflex. Now."

Farmer slowly stood up from the iron chair. He stepped around behind it, and walked to the other end of the cavern—he was about fifteen feet from me. Then, in an awkward gesture, he took that rock and threw it right square for my head.

The next second felt like a movie. Everything slowed down, it seemed, and I saw that rock coming straight for my face. The Farmer may be old, but he had an arm like a pitcher. I didn't have time to duck or anything. I didn't even have time to raise my arm. But I felt . . . something, without even meaning to—I had the instant thought that I didn't want that rock to hit me.

And it didn't.

About a foot in front of my face, the rock bounced off in the other direction like it had hit a rubber wall.

At that moment, I swore I was done—officially and truly done—doubting anything for the rest of my life. I was in a different world, I was crazy, I was in a coma—who knows, I thought, but, from then on, I might as well just accept things and go along with the ride.

Farmer walked up to me.

"Jimmy, as you grow accustomed to it, you will get better and better at controlling it. You will be amazed. It is not only a Shield, but it can be a weapon. You will learn when you need to. But The Shield goes beyond your thoughts. Your thoughts will control it much like they do your arm, but The Shield will do much more. It will protect you even when you do not know you need to be protected. Nothing, I mean nothing, my dear boy, that can harm you in any way, will get past The Shield. Nothing."

He leaned even closer.

"I daresay, Jimmy, my boy, you are now, without even the slightest hesitation, the most powerful person on the face of your entire world."

He let his words sink in. And they did.

"And this is only the First Gift. There are three more. And you must get them."

"Mister, what really is behind all this? Why in the world is it me? What's the purpose of the Gifts? What are the bad things you say are going to happen?"

Farmer sat back down on the iron chair. He looked up at me, and he suddenly looked as sad as a kitty with no mama.

"Jimmy, you must, and will, know everything. In time. But it is your path, and you must discover it. We can only give you the Four Gifts and what guidance that we can. The rest is up to you for now. Like our purposes in setting up the Legend of the Door, it is important for you to learn some things for yourself. You must grow with every piece of knowledge you obtain. I will not say you have been chosen, Jimmy, but you are now here. You are now the only one. But I will tell you what I can in the time that we have."

He paused, silent for what seemed like forever.

"There is a book. However you got here, therein lies your source to find the book. You must find it, and it will lead you to the remaining Three Gifts. You have been given something most precious.

"Jimmy, you must use these Gifts to save the world from what is coming."

His statement had no time to hit me like it should have at that moment.

Things started changing. The room became . . . cold, and darker. Everything seemed to get blurry—like it was . . . disappearing. Farmer was fading right before me.

I yelled out in fear.

"Mister, what do I do, where do I go!? What's happening?"

The room seemed to spin, and I felt dizzy. Things just kept fading in and out. I was getting panicky.

Farmer spoke once more, and then like so many other things in my recent life, just plain disappeared.

"Run, Jimmy. Your time is far shorter than I could've imagined. Run."

The ground was actually shaking. My panic turned right into pure terror. I decided I'd better heed the old Farmer's words and get the heck out of there. As I turned, and shot out the old wooden door I had come through, I heard one last blurt from Farmer, even though he was no longer there. I had heard the line before, and it gave me the shivers.

"The Stompers are coming."

✧CHAPTER 24✧
Wall of Darkness

The long passage with the torches was no different from the terrible state of the room I'd just run out of. Colors faded in and out, the ground shook like thunder, strange misty air swirled around my feet. Everything was hazy. I had the strangest feeling like I was in a place that was about to cease to exist—just like poor Farmer.

I ran.

But not very well. About every four seconds the ground shook violently, and it threw me to the ground the first couple of times. I got kind of used to it, and moved with more care. Something awful was happening, and I had no idea what.

So I just ran.

The mist continued to swirl. The torches continued to be there one second and then gone the next. The ground continued to shake.

I could have sworn the passage was never that long, but it stretched on and on. Finally, I caught sight of the bottom of the stone stairwell. I bolted faster and reached the stairs.

I looked behind me, and froze in fear.

The passage was not fading in and out any more. It was just plain fading out. Like a big wave of water, a . . .dark wall was moving towards me.

A wall of blackness, just like the blackness at the lake, but it was moving with alarming speed.

It was ... consuming the passage, heading straight toward me. I had no idea what was happening, but I didn't want to be present when the wall reached the stairs.

As I started up the stairs, I remembered counting them.

Seventy-two. Seventy-two stone steps.

I climbed as fast as I could. A great rushing sound rose behind me, like the wall of blackness was a huge tidal wave of destruction.

I made it up ten steps, then looked down the center hole of the stairwell, and could see the blackness rushing upward. It wasn't just black—it was pure dark, like some kind of Emptiness that was alive, that was growing darker the more it ate. And it was getting closer and closer. I resumed my flight up the stairs.

Twenty steps.

The roar of the Blackness got louder and louder. I could barely hear the sound of my footsteps.

Thirty steps.

My heart pounded so hard it hurt. I wanted to die.

Forty.

The air started to feel different. I couldn't breathe very well. It felt like a wind was blowing from above me—I thought the Blackness must be sucking everything into it.

Fifty.

I pounded up each step, pushing myself way beyond anything I ever thought I could do.

Fifty-five.

I could see the Blackness, right below me. It was almost to my feet.

Sixty.

Every breath killed. There was no air.

Ten more steps.

Something tugged at my feet. It felt like I had just stepped in glue. And then I heard the humming sound, the opening of the door above. From somewhere deep inside of me, a final push of strength burst out.

Every step was an effort, but I forced myself upward.

Five steps left. Four. Three.

I saw branches, I saw leaves . . .

I dove with every ounce of strength in my body, felt the soft earth and leaves as I landed.

There was another quick humming, and then all was dead silent.

✧CHAPTER 25✧

The First Gift

The only sound I could hear was me, panting.

I found myself lying on my back, looking up at the overhanging branches and leaves. If there was a moon out, I sure couldn't see it. I could barely make out anything it was so dark. And I was still breathing like a marathon-running dog. My heart beat a thousand miles a minute.

I slowly pulled myself up into a sitting position, and looked over at the Door.

Or where the Door *had* been.

It was gone.

I tore the flashlight out of my backpack to make sure. Right where the door had been, there was nothing but leaves and twigs. And they didn't even look flat like something had been lying there. It was just plain gone, and by the looks of it, had never been there in the first place.

I shone the light over at the keyhole in the twisted tree.

Gone.

What about the key? I thought in alarm. I looked all over, around and under the tree. I tore through the scattered leaves, looking desperately. It was gone, too.

The words of Farmer came back into my head. He had said that I wasn't really in the ground under the woods—that the Door was basically an entry into another world or dimension or whatever the heck you want to call it. I figured it didn't matter if I understood it or not—or else Farmer would have explained it more. He had also said that he was nothing but a messenger. Was that his version of a taped recording? Was the Door only an illusion or beacon—a sign to turn on the recording? All these thoughts went through my head, and I was still as clueless as before.

The Key.

The Door.

The Legend.

It was all gone—in the past now. The Door was gone!

But then I corrected myself. According to Farmer, this was only the beginning. I still had three Gifts to obtain. And it looked like I needed to go to Japan if I ever wanted to find out how to get them—at least I assumed that the book Farmer spoke about was the same one my dad sought out so long ago and had to leave there in Japan so he wouldn't burn up.

Then I remembered The Shield.

I wondered if it was really true. Or had I just finished the biggest hallucination in history? And if it was true, was it really as powerful as Farmer said it was?

Crazy.

I stood up, brushed myself off, and walked over to Ol' Betsy. I leaned my back against the big trunk of the tree, and stared out in to the night.

What in the world had my life turned into? I could never know again what to expect out of this world, because just when I think I'm comfortable with things, something like meeting a little girl in the middle of a cavern in the middle of the earth happens, followed by a fainting spell, followed by a Farmer telling me that I was now the most powerful person in the world.

More somber thoughts then entered my little head. Especially a certain phrase. I had heard it twice now.

The Stompers are coming.

I didn't know who or what a Stomper was, but I didn't like the sound of it.

Stompers.

It must have something to do with the Blackness that I had now seen several times. Blackness, sucking up life, delivering . . . Stompers? Who knew.

I thought back to the Shield. I thought of the other three Gifts. And finally, what Farmer had told me to do with them.

The Stompers are coming.

Save the world from what is coming.

I stood up from leaning on the tree, and took a deep breath. A small surge of strength came into me from somewhere, some sense of duty, I guess. Some feeling that I needed to quit feeling sorry for myself, quit asking questions that weren't going to be answered, and do what needed to be done.

Farmer had said that I needed to save the world.

Well, I thought, that's all fine and good, but first things first.

I needed to save my family.

✧ ✧ ✧

What else to do, I thought, but go to Raspy's house? I figured he either had my family there, or I would learn something valuable as to where he *did* have them.

It was getting very late by now—well after midnight. I took the long walk back through the woods, except this time I went towards my house. I thought I might as well check there, just in case they were hoping I'd come by and fall into their trap. I couldn't believe the faith I was already gaining in The Shield. It had only been tested by a rock thrown by an old farmer, but it had worked, after all. And I felt deep inside of me that I could trust the man who threw that rock. The messenger from who knows who. The Giver.

I came near the edge of the woods, and could see my house through the thinning branches. The front porch light was on, and there was a street lamp on the corner as well. As far as I could tell, there was no movement or anything outside or in. I decided to run up to it and take a look.

I shot across the street, creating a spooky, long shadow of myself running in the opposite direction. Thoughts of that first day came back in full force, when I had run across this same street in the opposite direction, looking for a tree to climb. I wondered what would have happened if I'd never gone that day.

I crouched next to the rosebushes my mom had by the driveway, and took another look.

Nothing.

I half crawled, half ran to the sidewalk leading up from the driveway, went around the corner of the house, and up to the front door.

It was open.

Barely open, but open. You could see a small, thin crack of light where it stood slightly ajar. I got the creeps. But I now had to go in.

I slowly pushed open the door, trying desperately not to make any sound. But that was impossible. That door was probably older than the Pope himself, and it creaked when I moved it. In the dark, silent night it sounded like I had just cranked up a chainsaw. I was sure that if there were bad guys in my house, they'd be on top of my skinny bottom before I even got through the door.

I hurried through and ran over to the living room couch, slid behind it, and listened for noises. Still nothing.

I was about to get up and do more exploring when I did hear a sound. It was very faint, but it sounded like a man talking—and it was coming from upstairs. I strained and strained, but couldn't hear what he was saying. It just sounded like somebody mumbling in his sleep.

Exactly when I became the bravest kid since Huckleberry Finn, I don't know, but I crept out from behind the couch and headed up the stairs. Halfway up, I could tell the sound was coming from my mom and dad's room, which was down the hallway once you made it upstairs. When I got to the top, I peeked in Rusty's room, and then mine.

Empty.

I crept to the door of my parents' room. It was closed, and there was a light shining from under the door. The mumbling voice had stopped.

My heart had barely recovered from The Door experience, but it started right back up again. I could almost hear it thumping. What was I supposed to do?

I knocked. Craziest thing in the world to do, but I knocked.

I heard footsteps approaching the door, I saw the door handle rotate.

Someone was opening the door.

I stepped back, and waited. It opened.

In the saddest voice I had ever heard come from his lips, he just said, "Oh, Jimmy, you shouldn't have come here."

It was Dad.

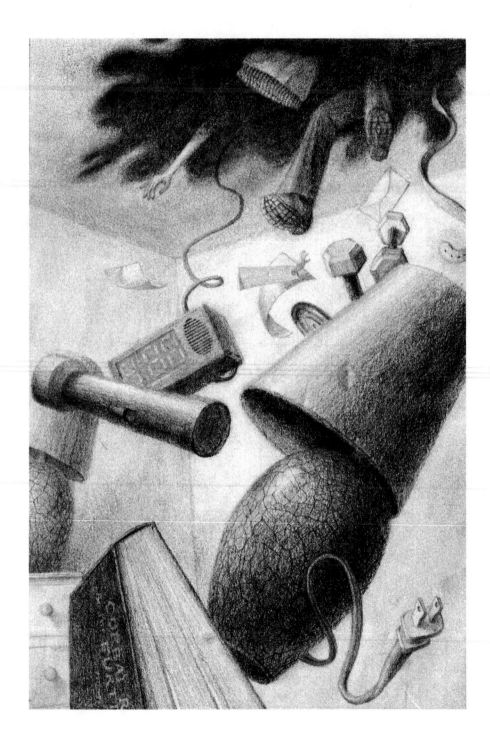

✧CHAPTER 26✧

Hello and Good-bye

The voice of my nightmares came from behind him. Raspy. Custer Bleak.

"Well, Jimmy, my boy, welcome home. Come on in and join us."

The door swung open all the way, and I saw what filled the room.

Mom and Rusty were on the bed, each with their hands tied or handcuffed behind their back. My dad had a rope around his neck, with Monster holding the other end of it—like my dad was a dog or something. More than anything else during this whole stupid thing, that made me downright ticked off like never before.

Raspy sat in the reclining chair my mom liked to sit in as she watched the TV. That old cuss had the nerve to have the footrest raised, sitting back with his feet up like he was king of the world. Monster jerked on the rope and Dad went over and sat by my mom.

Raspy spoke again.

"Jimmy, I know you have been through The Door. It enrages me, I'll admit, but yes, I know you have been there. I must say, you have slightly outmaneuvered me, but it is all well and good. We all know that The Door is only the beginning, and that there is still much more to look forward to.

"Tell me, Jimmy, what did you find there?"

There was no way I was giving up any secrets. I'm not the

best liar in the world, but I gave it a shot.

"Nothing. The Door opened, I went down some stairs, came back up, and the whole thing disappeared like it had never been there. Go look for yourself."

Raspy smiled at me. I couldn't believe how old that guy looked.

"Nothing, huh? Too bad. Too bad you are a bad liar. Jimmy, I know that you know that terrible things are abreast in the world. The world is changing, and certain things are going to happen soon that will make your childhood nightmares seem like Sesame Street. I want to fight it, Jimmy, and I want you to help me. Tell me what you found there, and we will all be better off."

I was trying to think. What could I do? What could I do!

An idea popped in my head.

"I saw the Stompers. They came before I was able to receive the Gifts. I barely escaped. It's over."

A look passed over Raspy's face—just for the smallest moment, but it was there. Surprise. Pleasant surprise. Creepy surprise.

"Stompers, eh? Tell me, what do they look like?"

Ummmmm . . .

"Like death." Corny as heck, but I hoped he'd go for it.

"You have no idea, little boy."

Raspy stood up and held his right hand in front of him. In his palm was a round, black ball. I couldn't tell what it was made of. It wasn't shiny, it wasn't dull, it was just a deep black. That scared me.

"Jimmy, the Black Curtain is ripping more and more each day. Slowly, randomly, but it is lifting. The Random Rippings are increasing. You will help us, or you will perish, along with your family. It is that simple. The old fools—the Givers—they have tried and tried to prevent the Black Curtain from lifting, but it looks like they are failing. If you've been given the power to stop the Stompers, I must say, it looks rather weak. And all the while, their power grows stronger. Until now, you and your family are only alive because you were of value to us. To help us discover the Legend of the Door. I know you have been there, and you *will* tell me everything. And I will now show you why. Unlike you, I *have* been given a gift."

He threw the black ball into the air above him, and it instantly spread out into a large, flat, black space, hanging over our heads. A wind suddenly sprang up in the room, a strong one that fed into the emptiness. The Blackness.

"Only I can rip the Black Curtain myself, whenever, wherever!" Raspy yelled.

The wind grew stronger. Small items from the room started flying into the Blackness. My family held onto the bed as tight as they could. I lost my footing and fell to the floor, then felt my feet jerked upwards, like somebody was pulling me. I grabbed for the leg of the dresser by the door and held tight.

I looked around me. My family could not fight it.

They were sucked into the Blackness, like loose paper into a vacuum cleaner, and disappeared.

I screamed. I looked at Raspy and Monster. It was not affecting them at all. They were laughing at me. Then Raspy reached up, and the Blackness instantly swarmed back into his hand, forming the same ball as before.

The wind stopped, and I slumped to the floor.

"Jimmy, my boy," said Raspy, "looks like your family went on a little trip! How about that? Just like that, and they're gone."

He came over to me, and crouched down.

"Jimmy, they are not dead. But they are in a very scary place. If you want them back, you will help me. Now, let's go to The Door, and see what we can see. Get him.""

Monster came over and reached for me. I felt something—an instinct, an instant thought. Monster's hands stopped in midair, two feet from my body, smashing into an invisible wall. He jumped back in shock, then lunged for me again. This time it not only repelled him, but threw him backwards. He landed on his back about ten feet away.

The Shield.

I quickly glanced at Raspy. The shock was on his face as well.

I jumped up.

"I've been through the Door. I've been given powers you could never even imagine. Bring back my family—NOW!"

Monster drew a gun and fired. Time seemed to slow once again. I could almost see the bullet flying.

I didn't want the bullet to hit me. So, it didn't. It ricocheted off The Shield and flew back at Monster, barely missing him, exploding the lamp on my mom's dresser. Monster's shock now turned into fear.

Raspy was the one to speak.

"I see you were lying after all, my young friend. Well, the plans may change, but the outcome will remain the same."

He threw the ball to his side now, and the Blackness appeared as a vertical wall this time.

"We will meet again, Jimmy. Remember, I have your family."

Before I could even react, he and Monster jumped into the Blackness, and it vanished.

Just like that, they were all gone.

I was alone. My family, gone.

I fell to the ground, and my body shook as I sobbed and sobbed.

✧CHAPTER 27✧

A Silvery Sea

By the next morning, I realized that I had cried myself to sleep.

Groggy, depressed, confused—I didn't know what I could possibly do for my family now.

After finding something to eat downstairs, I grabbed my backpack and just set off towards town. All I could do was wander, and think. And that's exactly what I did all day.

I didn't see anyone that I knew, I had no encounters with Raspy or his men, and I saw nothing that looked like a black curtain of darkness. It was a boring, and terrible day. I finally headed back home and went to sleep in my own bed for the night.

The next morning, I decided to take a walk back to where the door had been. Maybe it would be back, or maybe the Farmer or the girl would show up again to help me. I just didn't know what else to do.

The path across the street from my house looked the same as it always had. But on this day there was no excitement, no desire to climb trees, nothing. Everything had become a dull haze of loneliness.

As I headed for Ol' Betsy, I thought about some things that Raspy and Hairy had said. The Blackness obviously was the same thing as the Black Curtain, or at least very related. And Hairy had said that he hated using the "Random Rippings," instead of Raspy just coming to get him. And Raspy had said he was the only one who could rip it himself, "whenever, wherever." Was the Blackness a passageway from here to there, or was it much deeper than that? Where had it taken my family? What in the heck was it? Why—

Something got my attention, a ripping sound, and cut off my thoughts.

To my right, through several trees, back in the woods, I saw a shadow appear. Not a shadow. Blackness. Like it had read my thoughts, the Blackness had suddenly appeared. I was sure of it.

I ran towards it, and my initial thoughts were confirmed.

Hanging in the air, ten feet in front of me, was a wall of spilled ink—the Blackness. Something told me this was a Random Ripping of the Black Curtain, and that such luck just might not repeat itself.

I didn't even pause to think. I didn't pause to consider how stupid it would be to just up and jump into something that I had no idea what it even was. I didn't stop and think that maybe, just maybe, jumping into a wall of darkness meant certain death. I didn't think at all.

I simply took off towards the Blackness and jumped right into the middle of it.

✧ ✧ ✧

Everything immediately went dark—I could not see a thing, and there was no sign of a hole of light or anything else behind me. I had landed on solid ground, and all was black. There was no sound, and there was no wind. I was suddenly in the middle of nothing—absolute nothing.

Then things began to change. From somewhere a light started to glow, although I couldn't see the source. But I began to make out what was around me.

I was standing on a path of some sort, and it looked like

black marble. On both sides of the black path, only an inch or two below it, stretching far into the horizon, was an ocean of silvery, shining water, rippling with a sudden wind. The air was filled with mist—swirling, wet mist, like a thousand miniature clouds dancing all around the water and path. The black path wound away from me in both directions, winding this way and that into the distance, until it disappeared on both horizons.

The path was all I could see in that vast ocean of silvery liquid. There was nothing beside the path, above it, or below it. It just seemed to be floating on the water, and I was standing on it. I took a couple of coins out of my pocket and tossed them over the side. They splashed into the water, but it looked more like thick, shiny ink than water.

My mind once again brought up *The Wizard of Oz*, and Dorothy telling Toto that they weren't in Kansas anymore.

I was standing on a black path, on top of an ocean of silver. I wasn't in Georgia anymore, Toto.

Filled with wonder, excitement, and terror, all at the same time, I didn't know what else to do but to start walking.

I walked and I walked. Nothing changed. The path stretched forever, and I could still see nothing in either direction.

Then, finally, I saw something, way in the distance. It was way too small to figure out what it was, but I could sense movement, and that is was on the black marble path. After a few seconds, I could see that it was moving towards me, and it started to take shape. After a few more seconds, I realized it was moving fast. Very fast. Getting bigger and bigger, moving like a race car down the path, right at me.

I started to panic. I knew that I had come into a place of horror, and that this could not be something good. I started to walk backwards, timidly wondering what I could possibly do.

I could soon see it well. It was a dark shape, bounding along the path like some kind of animal. With it came the sound of a rushing wind. As it got closer, I could start to make it out better and then better, and panic ripped through me.

It was like a moving shadow. And it was huge—twice my size at least. I could see no features or anything—it seemed to be made of the same blackness of the gateways that led to this place. The shape of it was like a hunchback human, crouched over and using all four limbs to run. And it seemed to be wearing a hooded cloak or something—I could see it flapping in the wind as it ran. It was the strangest sight, because it seemed to be a shadow, but at the same time I could tell its shape. It wasn't long before none of that mattered. It was almost to me, bounding down the path like a crazed animal coming for its kill. I had the sudden thought that that was exactly what it was doing.

I turned and ran. I was scared beyond anything ever before—more than all the crazy stuff of the last few days. I panicked so bad that I started to shake, making it impossible to run. I suddenly tripped, slamming down onto the path, banging my head against the cool, hard marble surface. I flopped over on my back and looked up in terror.

The Shadow was almost on me. Ten feet away it jumped into the black air above me, and I could see it arch its cloaked, shadowy head into the air above it, and it let out a terrible scream. For a second, it was like it was just floating there. Then its head snapped back down, looking at me with eyes that I could not make out within the darkness of its horrible face.

Then it came straight down for me, arms reaching out like a vampire, ready to grab me and eat me alive.

Like it had hit a plastic bubble, its descent slowed suddenly two feet from my face. For a split second, the Shadow, with its flapping hood of darkness, stared straight into my eyes. Then it flew backwards violently, letting out another ear-piercing scream, and slammed down onto the path twenty yards in front of me.

Not for the first time, and most definitely not for the last, I had been saved by The Shield.

I quickly sat up and started to scoot backwards along the path, like the old crabwalk race we used to do in elementary school. The Shadow stood up, and once again flew at me like a raging beast.

This time, it bounced off of me even harder, and flew out to the side of the path. I quickly glanced over at it, and watched as it fell into the mercurial waters. I slid over to that side of the path and grabbed the edges of it, looking where it had fallen. Through the swirling mists, it was hard to see, but I saw the Shadow get swallowed up by the silver ocean, screaming the entire time.

I flopped over onto my back and stared at the air above me, panting heavily. I couldn't believe what I had just seen. It started to hit me the more I calmed down. Until now I had seen terrible men and terrible things, but now I had seen something that truly and finally proved that there were monsters in the world, that every kid's nightmares were not fantasy after all. That not only do we have to deal with evil men and black holes that eat people, but with real, bona fide monsters.

I tried not to think about the fact that my family was hidden somewhere in this terrible place.

Without The Shield.

✧Chapter 28✧

Iron Rings

I soon started walking again. *I have no idea where this path could possibly lead, but surely it has to go somewhere,* I continued to tell myself.

I walked and I walked. Nothing changed.

A while later, I again saw a black figure approaching from the distance. The same shape, the same hunched over, bounding motion. The same hooded cloak flapping in the wind. I got scared, but nothing approaching the panic of the first Shadow monster.

I decided I would just kneel down and wait this time. The Shield was for real, I was getting more and more sure of it. Besides, what else was there to do?

Closer and closer it came. A scream ripped through the air. I worked desperately not to get up and run, fought all of my instincts. I kept my own screams inside, held onto my faith in The Shield. I stayed put, kneeling before the Shadow like it was my new king, staring straight at it. It was probably the hardest thing I'd ever done up to that point in my life.

It jumped into the air, and came for me.

Time slowed, The Shield rebounded, and another Shadow monster fell into the ocean of silver, with the same desperate screams.

I let out the breath I'd been holding for thirty seconds, and collapsed onto my hands and knees. I swore right then that I would never again doubt the power I now had. The

Shield. I no longer had reason to fear anything, and I needed to understand that if it was truly going to help me like it should.

I continued my walk. Three more Shadow beasts came, all with the same result. I no longer kneeled, or crouched, or anything. I just kept walking, not even giving those things the satisfaction of seeing me scared. They bounced into the ocean—all of them.

That path led me, both literally and figuratively, to the sure knowledge that Farmer was right—I was now the most powerful person in the world. At least in the sense that not even big Shadow beasty things could hurt me.

And then thoughts of my family again flooded my head, and sobered me right up.

I walked on.

I don't know if it was hours and hours, or maybe even a whole day. It was forever to me. But finally, I came upon something different, and even though I was clueless as to what it was, it seemed a welcome sight.

I first noticed it when I was still far off. I immediately thought it was another Shadow coming to meet its doom, but quickly realized it wasn't moving. I could just tell there was something there. As I got closer, it started to take shape, although it sure didn't help me figure out what it was. In fact, when I got to within two feet of it, I still didn't know. I sat there and stared at it, and wondered what it could be.

The path branched out into a wide, circular area, probably about the size of a large room in your typical house. On the other side of the circle, the path shot out and continued on forever and ever. I couldn't believe what a strange place this was.

The circle wasn't made out of the black marble. It was a dark stone—just like the stone that made up the stairs and stuff under The Door. And it was polished perfectly smooth.

There was something in the middle of that circle.

It was a stack of iron rings, about three feet across in diameter. Nothing fancy, just a series of circular iron rods, connected by little beams of some kind of other metal, stacked up until it reached about my waist, making what looked like a barrel with no top. That was it. A big slab of smooth stone with a barrel of iron rings in the middle.

I walked up to it, and looked inside of it. I couldn't really see much. I took out the trusty flashlight and shined it inside. Nothing, it was totally empty—the inside looked just like the outside, with the bottom being the same stone floor as I was standing on.

I stepped back and wondered what could possibly be the purpose of such a thing.

I didn't have to wonder long.

There was a sudden flash of light, as if an explosion had just ripped through the bottom of the iron rings, bursting out of the top, blinding me. I fell to the ground.

Then, the light was gone. As I tried to adjust my eyes, everything was blurry for a few seconds. I could tell there was a man standing inside the iron rings, immediately making the hairs on my neck shoot for the sky.

I remember seeing a movie once about a boy who saw dead people. All my friends told me that it had a surprise ending, and I remember thinking that just knowing that it had a surprise ending would make it so that it wasn't that great of a surprise. But when the movie did end, lo and behold, I was completely shocked.

This was kind of like that. Just when I thought that I was beyond being surprised or shocked by anything again—because I had accepted the fact that anything was possible—I saw a man standing in an iron barrel, looking at me. Out of all the people it could have been, it surely was the one I could have never guessed.

Standing in front of me, dressed in the same crazy clothes I'd last seen him in, was a man that I knew to be dead.

Joseph.

✧CHAPTER 29✧

Him . . . Again

I couldn't do a thing but stare. He was dead. I'd seen him die.

He could tell I was about to go in shock.

"Jimmy, buddy, good to see ya. You really must be about to poop in your pants wondering what in the heck I'm doing alive, much less what I'm doing here of all places. Well, I'm not dead, and I am here, and we've got a lot to do."

Joseph stepped out of the iron rings and walked over to me. He put his hand on my shoulder and squeezed. Well, he wasn't a ghost. But seeing him made me look like one, I was sure.

"Jimmy," he said, "come over here and sit down on the ground with me. I want to tell ya a couple of things to convince you that you're not due to check into the loony bin tonight."

We went over near the edge of the stone circle and sat down, facing each other. I was really hoping to be enlightened by crazy, used-to-be-dead Joseph. Still too shocked to even speak, I had to compose myself and finally got out some words.

"Joseph, I saw you that night. You were covered in blood, and I swore I saw your last breath come out of you."

"I know, Jimmy, I know. But this place does amazing things to you. This . . . place. That old hairy son of a gun sent me here as soon as he could, to get rid of me, to hide any trace of his murdering ways. Well, I wasn't quite as dead as he or you thought. I woke up here, in the Blackness, and knew I was barely alive. But I suddenly started to heal—like it was magic or something. I can't explain it, but I'm not kidding ya—this place heals people. Or at least it did me. Couldn't of been more than a couple of hours and I was completely whole again—there wasn't a scrape on me. What happened to all those shotgun pellets, who knows? Maybe they're still inside of me. But the point is, dang it if I'm not alive! I'm alive, Jimmy, and I've been exploring this place ever since trying to find my way out."

I rocked back and put my arms around my knees, and tried to soak in all that Joseph had said. I'd thought he was dead, but he wasn't quite dead, but then he was almost dead, and then he got sent here and now he's not even close to dead. Whatever, nothing was ever going to surprise me again—I'd sworn it.

"Fine, Joseph, I'm real glad you're not dead. What do we do now?"

"Well, I've learned a few things about this place. It's some kind of passageway between worlds or dimensions or something like that. Every few miles, you'll see this same kind of stone circle with the iron rings in the middle. The rings serve as some kind of gate to different . . . places. Worlds, I think. I can only tell you that some of the places I've seen are not earth. Or, I'm as crazy as you can get. I don't know, but you wouldn't believe the things I've seen since I came here."

"What about the shadow things—the shadow monsters? Haven't you seen any of those?"

Joseph suddenly got a look on his face like the death that he had somehow just escaped.

"You mean the Shadow Ka."

We were both quiet for a second or two, like he had just revealed the murderer in a bad made-for-TV mystery movie.

"Yeah, I guess. How did you survive those things?"

"The Givers saved me."

"Givers?"

"Yeah, the Givers. They saved my poor skinny runt, and then took me to one of the stone gates. They said that they were running out of time, and told me to run, to get away. Ever since, I've been jumping through a few of these gates and haven't seen a Shadow Ka since. Once was enough, I tell you."

I realized that the more Joseph talked, the less I understood the situation.

"Joseph, please just start from the beginning and tell me everything."

"Okay, but quickly. Like I said, I was dead to the world up in that cabin in Utah. I could sense Dontae dragging me somewhere, but just barely, like I was in a dream. Then I remember hearing this strange sound, like a tearing, ripping sound, and then I could feel myself being heaved through the air. I remember landing on a hard surface, and pain just ripping through my body. I think I passed out. But then I came to and realized I wasn't dead. And I could . . . *feel* my body healing. It wasn't long before I was brand new.

"But then I thought I had gone crazy or was just plain dead because I was in heaven or hell. There I stood, on a black path in the middle of a misty, silvery ocean. I started walking, not having the slightest clue as to where I could possibly be or where I was going. And then came the Shadow Ka, and I knew I was in hell, and I started wondering what I'd done in life that was so bad."

Joseph was getting shaken up remembering the terror of the shadow beast. I didn't blame him. I asked him a quick question.

"How do you know that's what they're called—'Shadow Ka'? Did you make that up?"

"No, the Givers told me, but I'm getting to that. Just give me a minute."

He gathered his thoughts and then continued.

"That beast of a shadow came at me like a starving lion on a wildebeest. I fell to my knees and threw my hands up, waiting on death—so soon after I'd thought I'd just escaped it. But then I saw a flash of light and I glanced up and saw the Ka falling in the ocean to my right. And ahead of me, on the path, were standing two . . . people. You really must be thinking I've lost it Jimmy, but you ain't heard nothing yet. Standing in front of me, with concerned but kind faces, were an old farmer and a little girl. I swear it, Jimmy."

Farmer, and the little girl who had told me it was "about time, Jimmy Fincher." Wow, I thought. Who *were* those people?

"Joseph, I'll tell you my story before long, I'm sure, but trust me—I believe you."

He gave me a suspicious look before he continued.

"They called themselves the Givers, or that they were from a people called the Givers. And they told me basically to shut up and follow them. We ran down the black path until we came up on one of these stone circles with the iron rings, and they took me through one. Suddenly, we were in the strangest place I ever saw—even stranger than a black path in the middle of nowhere.

"The air around me was filled with a moist, biting cold, and there was almost no light—enough to see, but very, very dim. Above me, far off in the distance, I could make out a dark, cloudy, gray . . . something. I couldn't tell if it was the sky or a massive ceiling. It just looked like the darkest, meanest storm clouds you ever saw. Then I looked around me.

"In every direction, for as far as I could see, stood a sea of stone beds—hundreds, thousands of beds, spaced roughly ten feet apart, each bed with someone dressed all in gray, lying flat on their back. As far as I could tell, they were all asleep. Or dead. And then I noticed that the bodies on the stone beds were not quite human—they were way too big, and just not shaped quite the same. Like I said, it was pretty dark.

"The Givers told me that this was a world that used to be as alive and as happy as ours. That the dark clouds hanging over us had replaced a beautiful green sky with two suns, and that the plants and wildlife on this planet had been beyond anyone's imagination of what beauty was. But now, this was all that was left. An entire world and civilization brought to this by the . . ."

Joseph trailed off, and I urged him to continue.

"The Stompers, Jimmy, this is what the Stompers do to worlds. They destroy it, but keep the people barely alive to fulfill some purpose that no one understands. That's why they build the stone beds. It's beyond horrible, Jimmy—the most horrific thing I've ever seen. I asked them why they had brought me there.

"This place we've been calling the Blackness, well, it's been around for literally millions of years. It's a pathway between . . . worlds and dimensions. Why it's here, where it came from? No one really knows. It's just here. But the Givers didn't have time to go into too much detail. They said they just wanted me to experience firsthand the danger that threatened our little world we like to call Earth. They said that the Stompers were coming.

"You see, these stone and iron gateways—there's one for every world that exists in the universe, and for every dimension. I'm not totally sure what all that means, but that's what they said. But anyway, for some reason, there has never been a gateway to earth. Again, no one knows why—but somehow, a gate to earth was never . . . created, or built, or whatever.

But once long ago the Givers discovered something that they realized might be their last hope to stop the Stompers. They said they discovered a way to tear the Blackness—they called it the Ripping of the Black Curtain. And every time they tore it, it led to earth. They decided, that if nothing else, they could save earth, and hope against hope that one day we'd return the favor.

"The Givers knew that if they could rip the Curtain, eventually the Stompers would learn how to do it. So they came to our world, and prepared a way. They knew the chances were slim, but there was only so much they could do. And that's where the whole Legend of the Door business came about—everything from the book in Japan to the Door in Duluth. The Givers did it all. But it wasn't long before their fears were realized and the Stompers did tear the Black Curtain.

Well, that is to say, the Shadow Ka tore the Curtain. I guess they're the servants of the Stompers and have to prepare the way for them. For some reason, the Stompers cannot come until those Shadow Jerks have 'prepared the way,' whatever in tarnations that means. The Givers didn't say much about that stuff.

"Anyway, I guess a Shadow Ka can literally enter and control someone's mind—that's actually the only way they *can* enter another world. So, that's what they did to visit our sweet little planet. And Jimmy, I don't believe I gotta tell you who they decided to use as their earthly hotel."

"Raspy," I whispered.

✧CHAPTER 30✧

Shadow Ka

My mind couldn't quit spinning, my eyes looking off into nowhere, my understanding only scratching the surface of truths that were way beyond any thing I could have ever dreamed or made up.

"Right-o, brother," Joseph continued. "Custer Bleak and all of his cohorts, I'm sure. I bet they're all controlled by the Shadow Ka, Jimmy. And from the beginning they've been trying to figure out the Legend of the Door before some good kid like yourself could stumble on it and help save the world. Ironic, ain't it? If it wasn't for their efforts, me, your dad, and you would have never even known about the whole thing. I bet those crazy fools have a few regrets. And I bet when they report back to the Stompers, whoever in the heck they are, they're going to get a good tongue-lashing, eh?"

I couldn't help but look at Joseph in wonder—how could he take all this so trivially and make small jokes? If all this garbage was true, what did it mean for our world, for our families, for our future? I felt more confused than when he started.

"So let me get this straight," I said. "This place is a pathway between worlds. The Stompers are some evil creatures that go around and destroy these worlds—or at least most of it, anyway. But, lucky for us, there was no iron-ring gate to earth, so they haven't ever done a thing to us. Until the Black Curtain was ripped, which leads to our world. Then

138

the Givers set up a way to help us, and the Stompers sent the Shadow Ka to figure it out before the humans did."

"You got it, good buddy." Joseph actually smiled.

I slumped onto my back and stared up into nothing. I felt like I had just given a quick movie review for the worst movie ever made. At least the most hard-to-swallow movie ever made.

"Joseph, who in the world are the Givers?"

"Now, that, I don't rightly know. They don't like to talk about themselves too much. But from what I hear from the Farmer and his daughter, or whatever and whoever they are, you, Jimmy Fincher, are now one special little guy. You did it, didn't ya? You found the key, you opened the Door?"

"Yeah. I did."

"Wow, Jimmy. All I can say is wow. I guess I never really and truly believed that it was all for real. But, I ain't got nary a doubt now. The Givers told me a little about what you found there—about the Four Gifts and such. Unbelievable. Little snotty-nosed Jimmy Fincher who used to beg me to play Lincoln Logs is now the most powerful human to ever walk the earth."

"Shut up, Joseph. How come you didn't tell me about the year my dad went to Japan? I don't remember a thing about you living with us that year."

"Yeah, I know. Going to the cabin that night, I just didn't want to tell ya anything that sounded too crazy. I wanted to let you in on it slowly. If I'd told you that your dad went to Japan and we were looking to open a magic door and had a special key hidden in a statue of an elephant, how do you think you would've reacted? I had to let you in slow and build trust—because I knew your dad hadn't told you anything."

"I guess so. By the way, before you keeled over, you could've told me that it was an elephant, not a tree."

"It's a wee bit difficult to think clearly when you you've

just been blown up by a shotgun."

We both smiled, and for just a second, it almost felt like we were sitting on the grass at the ballpark, watching a little league game and shooting the breeze. Somehow, I had relaxed a little with Joseph letting a couple of jokes fly out.

"Well, Jimmy," Joseph said after a couple of minutes, "I know there's still a lot of questions that we're clueless on. I still don't have the slightest idea as to what a Stomper is. Or what in the heck you and your Four Gifts are going to do about them. Or why they send the Shadow Ka and not themselves. But, I guess we're learning inch by inch.

"Anyway, after the Givers showed me that world of drudgery, they told me as much as they could, and then just up and left. They said they had vital business to attend to back on earth. And that was you. That's probably the biggest mystery of all, Jimmy. They knew you were coming. They told me about you and the Gifts and everything *before* they went to meet you behind the Door. So that, I don't get. But, ever since they left me, I've been wandering around this crazy place looking for your family."

I jumped up.

"What? You know about my family? How—Where—"

"Calm down, now. Who do ya think told me? The Givers. I don't know where those folks came from, but they sure seem to know a lot. They said that Custer, or Raspy, brought your family here as ransom—to ensure they had a snare for you. Well, I found them."

"You did! Where? Let's go!" I was frantic.

"It ain't going to be that easy, Jimmy. We've got to put our thinking caps on and figure out how we're going to do this. Because us going to rescue them is exactly what the bad guys expect us to do. So we can't just lolly-dolly in there and pick 'em up and go. We've got to think."

I sat back down on the cold stone and looked at Joseph.

He stared at the ground and said nothing.
It was then that we heard the flapping sound.

✧CHAPTER 31✧

Cold

Joseph and I swiveled around and looked behind us, out into the mist. Coming straight at us, in what looked like the meanest, blackest thundercloud ever, was a pack of Shadow Ka. At least, they looked just like the Ka I had fought off before—except for one difference.

These had wings. Or maybe those wings were what I had thought was some kind of cloak. Shadowy beasts with wings.

And there were over a hundred of them, if not a thousand. We couldn't tell because the cloud of Ka seemed to stretch forever behind them, like a gathering hurricane ready to attack the South Carolina coast. The flapping of their wings made a strange, eerie sound—like a wet sheet flapping on a clothesline. And here and there the screeching sound of their screams pierced the misty, damp air.

We both fell back onto our bottoms in fright, and then scrambled up shouting to each other for suggestions on what in the heck to do.

They were coming in fast, and the closer they got, the louder the flapping and the screams became, and the more scared senseless we became. The Ka were probably a couple of football fields away then, and time was disappearing fast.

"Quick," yelled Joseph over the terrifying sounds of the flying Ka, "Jump into the iron rings!"

I didn't hesitate. I ran to the rings, grabbed the top edge and jumped over it into the cylinder of the gateway. Joseph then did the same, making a tight squeeze with both of us in there. The Ka were almost on us, maybe fifty yards, and seemed to be getting faster.

"What now?" I yelled.

"Just wait! It just happens!" Joseph yelled back. It was like the flapping of the shadow wings caused a great wind to come up—like there really was a hurricane on us.

Closer and closer. Their screams now were unbearable, and my ear drums were ready to explode. I was so terrified—despite finally remembering that I had the Shield. *But what about Joseph?*, I thought. *And can it really rebuff a million flying, screaming monsters?*

They arrived above us, and gathered into a tight pack of shadows, grouping tighter and tighter until they seemed to be one big, nasty, writhing beast. And then they dove, all at once, straight towards us.

I screamed. Joseph screamed. We were both drowned out by the shrieks of the Ka.

Ten feet. Five feet. Then countless claws of shadow were reaching out to tear our heads off.

There was suddenly a flash of light. And they all disappeared.

✧ ✧ ✧

The Shadow Ka had been replaced by snowflakes.

Just like everything else in my topsy-turvy life, it made no sense, but we were suddenly looking up into a million snowflakes—huge, pillowy flakes, coming out of a gray sky.

Quickly, I looked around us. We were no longer on a stone circle hovering in a strange world of mist and rain. We were in a world of whiteness—snow in every direction, for as far as we could see. And we were still standing in iron rings in the middle of that field of deep snow.

And it was very cold.

Joseph leaped out of the rings and urged me to do the same.

As I did, I asked him what on earth just happened.

"Just like I told ya, Jimmy, we went through a gate. We're now in the same place I had just come from before I bumped into you. It's very cold here."

Joseph certainly had no need to let me in on that whopper of a secret. I could already feel my nose freezing up and my face getting cold burn from the snow and slight wind. Not to mention I was wearing shorts and a T-shirt. And that I had seen snow about as much as I had seen Japanese snow monkeys. But the relief of getting away from the Shadow Ka overcame my shock and cold.

"Come on, Jimmy, there's a forest just over that rise, and an abandoned cottage-like place. I slept there last night, and I bet the coals from my fire are still burning."

In awe once again of the fairy tale that had become my life, I numbly jumped out of the rings and followed Joseph.

The snow was calf-high, and it was miserable to walk in. My legs became numb in minutes, and my ears and hands actually started to hurt terribly from the cold. The wind seemed to pick up, and the snow started to beat against my face like a million flies racing for some picnic food. It hurt, and I started thinking that maybe Shadow Ka weren't so bad after all. At least the Shield protected me from them.

The instant I had the thought, the snow started bouncing away from me, inches before my face. I no longer felt the icy wind against my body. The snow I was trudging along in became easier to walk through, and when I looked down, I was shocked to see that huge holes were forming for my legs and feet as I moved them. And I was suddenly nice and warm.

The Shield was actually repelling the snow and wind and cold. I realized it would never cease to surprise or amaze me. I had only thought of it as protecting me from dangerous projectiles like rocks and bullets. But the Shield was turning out to be an umbrella, heater, and snow shovel as well. Truly, I was one protected little guy. Amazing, absolutely amazing.

Joseph couldn't really tell what was happening because the thick snow was blinding, and he could barely concentrate on moving forward.

We trudged on, my journey a little easier than poor Joseph's.

We soon went over a rise and a deep, green forest loomed in a valley below us. It was so beautiful I felt like collapsing in wonder. The trees were mostly pine—shaped like Christmas trees—but bigger than any trees I had ever seen. They shot toward the sky like rockets, and the snowy trim on their branches just took my breath away. It was like I was looking at some kind of fantasy winter wonderland thought up and painted by a committee of the greatest artists ever known to man. It didn't seem real, and for a while I forgot our troubles.

We rushed down the snowy slope and were soon walking under the huge, mountainous trees. The bed of the forest ground was soft and mushy, making no sound as we walked. There wasn't much snow because of the tree cover, and there was an echo-y silence that was almost like the Blackness. And it seemed a lot warmer. I just couldn't imagine where we could possibly be, but I sure loved it.

"Jimmy," Joseph called out, breaking the silence like a loud sneeze in the middle of a cathedral. "The cottage is right up there, down that little path. Let's hurry—I'm about to freeze to death."

With no complaints from me, we did as he said, and soon

came upon what he kept calling the cottage.

I could see why he had chosen that word.

I was once again reminded of a painting—the kind that seemed to be almost too popular, sold in every store that could even remotely get away with selling art. I had seen what looked like the same painting a million times—an old-fashioned, brick home with warm lights glowing out of every window, completely surrounded by every flower in the book and little streams with stone bridges and fountains and all that other fancy stuff. I had always thought of the houses in those paintings as cottages.

Well, then Joseph and I were looking at a genuine cottage.

There were no lights coming through the windows, and there were no flowers, but it was the same kind of house. And it was beautiful, with the greener than green trees surrounding it and the snow lightly covering the roof. It really did look like a painting, and I wondered if we had somehow gone into a make-believe world completely controlled by a bunch of big-haired painters with funny, soft voices that did specials on PBS.

We ran up to the large, wooden door and Joseph opened it without hesitating.

The cottage was pretty empty inside, like it had been abandoned for years. There was no furniture or paintings on the walls or carpet or anything. It was just a bunch of wooden floors and white walls, and there was a lot of dust.

"Come back here through the hall, to the fireplace," said Joseph.

He ran ahead of me, and I yelled at him to wait up, then followed.

I trotted down the creaky old wooden floor of the hallway, past a big stairwell that went upstairs, and into a large living room. A roaring fire was burning in the big stone fireplace, and there was a small wooden table with some plates and food on it. Over the fire was a little iron rack, where I could tell someone had been cooking the meat that was now on the table.

But food was the last thing that I cared about when I saw what was there, sitting around that small wooden table on old stumps brought in from the forest.

Jumping up to greet me, yelling out a million things at once, were the three people in the world that made the blood flow through my veins and made my life worth living.

Mom, Dad, and Rusty.

In an abandoned cottage in the middle of a green forest blanketed with snow, in a world that wasn't my own, I fainted for the second time in my life.

✧CHAPTER 32✧

Catching Up

I woke up with my head in Mom's lap, and Dad gently tapping me on the face.

"Jimmy? Jimmy?" my dad kept asking.

It was the sweetest sound I'd heard in a long, long time.

I came to, and groggily sat up. My mom, Dad, and Rusty all gave me the biggest hugs in the history of the world, and for that brief moment, there wasn't a thing wrong in my life.

Then the questions started pouring out of me.

It turned out that Joseph had found these guys here, in this cabin, led there by the Givers, who had also led my family there. Once again, the question of who in the heck the Givers were was brought to mind. They always disappeared almost as quickly as they came. But there was no doubt as to whose side they were on, and for right then that was all that mattered.

My family had been in the Blackness ever since Raspy first threw them in there from my parents' bedroom a couple of nights ago. As soon as they were on the black path, they had been blindfolded, and taken to an iron gate, where they were then sent through the iron rings to a terrible place that smelled musty and dank. They were taken to a creepy, dirty, cave-like room, except it had been made out of some type of dark glass or crystal, with weird formations coming out of the walls. Their blindfolds had been removed, some food was left, and then Raspy and his hounds disappeared, promising to come back with me, or not at all.

Then the Givers had appeared, and my family shared the same shock that good ol' Joseph and I had felt when all of a sudden a little girl and an old farmer appeared out of nowhere. They had been led through several tunnels and caverns, all made out of the same dark crystal-like substance, until they came upon an iron gate, and re-entered the Blackness. They were then led here, as was Joseph, and they had an unusual, but happy, reunion.

The Givers then left, with no real explanation of what my family should do next.

So Joseph had used some hunting skills he'd learned—as a bona fide redneck—and they'd been eating rabbits and deer for three or four days.

They finally decided that one of them should go back into the Blackness and do something. Do what, they had no idea, but do *something*.

It was decided that Joseph should go. There was no way that my dad was going to leave his family again.

Joseph went to the iron rings, entered the Blackness, and lo and behold there I was, waiting on the stone circle like I'd been expecting him. I commented that the phrase "small world" applied to the Blackness as well. Somehow, someway, we were all back together again.

"Joseph, what was all that garbage about how we couldn't rush into things and we needed to think how we were going to rescue them and all that?" I asked, kind of miffed but not really.

"Ah, you know. I figured I'd give you a nice little surprise. I said to myself, 'that little guy deserves a nice, happy surprise to make up for all the ugly ones he's had in the last little while.' So, here you are."

He gave me his goofy smile, and I smiled back. But then

I went over and punched him in the gut.

I suddenly remembered that my dad had been shot in the leg, and I asked about it. It turned out the Blackness healed him just like it had Joseph. Even back at my house, when I had come back from going through the Door, I hadn't thought about why he wasn't hurt anymore. Life must really be upside down when you so quickly forget that your dad has been shot. Raspy must have taken them into the Blackness at least once before the episode in my parents' room.

"Well," Rusty said after a while, "Now what are we going to do? We've been so wrapped up in this unbelievable reunion, I almost forgot that we're in the middle of a forest in another world with a lot of people who want us dead. What on earth do we do now?"

I spoke up.

"First, I need to tell you guys things. I know we've all been through a lot of stuff that doesn't even begin to make sense, but I think we're also starting to finally accept the fact that the world is a little different from what we'd always thought it was. Especially me, Mom, and Rusty. Dad and Joseph, I guess you two have been learning that lesson, slowly but surely, for quite some time now."

They both nodded, but didn't say anything. I went on.

"Anyway, I think maybe things are even crazier than even you all might believe right now. I've been dying to get all this off my chest, so I think it's high time I filled you in on my last few days. I barely believe it all myself, so I guess you might believe it even less, but here goes."

I could tell they were anxious to hear what in the heck I was talking about—they didn't say a word, but sat down on the stumps, and waited for my story.

I told them everything. I didn't leave out one detail. How I found the key in Old Willow's trunk—Mom couldn't believe I'd forgotten her story about the famous elephant of Duluth,

Georgia—how I went to the Door, how I finally opened it, and what I found below. The girl, and the Farmer. I could tell that after entering the Blackness and coming to this strange place, they didn't really find my story that crazy after all.

Until I told them about the golden cup and the First Gift, the Shield, and Farmer's story about the other Three Gifts. About me being the most powerful person on the planet. About me saving the world. About the Stompers.

Things clicked in Dad's head, in Joseph's head, even in my head as I heard myself explain the whole thing. Things were starting to at least make a little sense, despite the complete whacked-out craziness of it all. Dad had told me in the car on our cross-country trip about the Stompers, and even though we didn't know what or who they were, we knew that they were the enemy, that they were a fierce enemy, and that they were "coming," whatever that meant.

The Stompers are coming.

That phrase gave me goose bumps every time I thought about it or said it.

And of course, poor Mom and Rusty, they were in no way, shape, or form prepared for all this information. At least for my dad and Joseph, and for me to an extent, it had been learned gradually. For them it had been like making a snow-cone out of an avalanche. They were silent, afraid, in shock. I wished so badly that we could all escape this mess and go back to the good ol' days.

I don't know if they really believed my entire story, at least right then. It was just too much—a fourteen-year-old boy from Duluth, Georgia given the first of Four Gifts, all in preparation for saving the world from something called the Stompers. I guess none of us really believed it all. As things got weirder and stranger, we didn't really think of things in those terms anymore—as believing it or not believing it. Things kind of went through your ears and into your brain, and were put aside until further notice. It was all just too much for the old brain to compute all at once.

The story-telling and reunion and useless attempts at planning what to do next went on for hours. I finally started to realize that I was more exhausted than I'd ever been before, and wanted to sleep for about the next hundred years. Everyone else felt the same, and we were surprised to see that it had grown dark outside, without us even noticing.

"Well," Dad said, "the sleeping arrangements aren't too sweet, but let's get some shut-eye. Grab a piece of floor, and get some sleep."

I went over to the corner of the room, near the fireplace, and curled up with my back against the wall, facing the rest of my family. I was dead-tired, and knew that sleep would hit me pretty quickly.

Dad obviously wasn't so raring to fall asleep right away, and kept talking.

"Ya know," he said, "I don't know quite what that old farmer-guy meant, but he told me that when we all finally do leave this place, to make sure that we 'block the Black Curtain.' He said that you were the only one that could do it, Jimmy. In fact, he said that you were the only person in existence, *anywhere*, that could block the Black Curtain. And that you must use the First Gift to do it. I can't even believe I remember what he said, because at the time it didn't make one ounce of sense. But now, I guess he was talking about that Shield thing of yours, huh?"

"Yeah, I guess." I mumbled, way too tired to register much of what he was saying.

As we all settled in and drifted off, Dad's last statement kind of went in one ear and out the other, and didn't seem like all that much at the time.

It would prove to make all the difference in the world in the months to come.

✧CHAPTER 33✧
Trouble

I woke up freezing, and could hardly stand it until Dad finally got a fire going again. I figured that the Shield only protected me from the cold when it approached a dangerous level, like it had been out in the snow. Whatever the reason, all I knew was that I woke up cold. As we huddled around the fire and ate some cold meat from the night before, it was almost like we were just on a normal excursion to a national park, sitting around the fire, getting ready for another day's fun.

Everyone was mostly silent, with small conversations about our predicament breaking out here and there. We were all anxious to get moving and scared silly at the prospect at the same time. Where would we go? What would we do? How would we fight off the Shadow Ka and Raspy and whoever else came at us? What if . . . the Stompers came?

It wasn't long before we knew we couldn't just sit there forever. Now that we were all together, there was no longer any reason to stay still. Once again, it was time to get moving.

We decided to go back to the iron gate, and re-enter the Blackness. We couldn't imagine there was anything in this cold place that would end up helping us. We hoped that maybe we would run into the Givers again, and they could lead us back through a ripping in the Black Curtain, back to our home.

We left the cottage just an hour or so after waking up. The air outside was still crisp with morning air, and at first it felt refreshing and really squeezed out all the grogginess from my bones. But after only a short while of walking, that cold started to bite again like it had the night before. And it was still snowing, although not much of it made it through the thickness of those unbelievably green trees.

Soon we came out of the forest, and back into the huge field of snow. This time it was even deeper, and each step became a major chore. Especially for me, the only one of us wearing shorts. My skin started to feel numb again, and I couldn't wait for the iron rings.

It wasn't long before the Shield kicked in like it had the day before, and I was suddenly nice and comfy again. We went over the rise of the valley wall and entered the long, flat field of white before us, and could make out the iron rings in the distance. The sight of it encouraged us, and we trudged on even harder. The snow pelted everyone but me, and this time Joseph noticed it, as did my family.

I told Mom to come over by me, and I put my arm around her and walked as close to her as I could. I wanted to try an experiment.

It worked. In fact, it worked far better than I had hoped.

The Shield immediately expanded, and rebounded the snow, wind, and cold off the both of us. My mom was bewildered—she just couldn't believe it was real. I was again taken aback at the possibilities of this amazing Gift I had been given.

I soon called Rusty over. He put his arms around my mom. It didn't work.

I told him to come over to my other side and he then put his arm around me, so that I looked like a linebacker being helped off the field by his brother and mom after a brutal block. The Shield then expanded, and all three of us were now protected from the biting snow.

Joseph came over and kind of put his arms around my neck from behind. We looked awkward, but suddenly my dad was the only one getting pelted with snow.

Joseph broke away and went back over to walking with my dad. No one really said anything—they were all just stunned at the weirdness of the Gift I had. They couldn't believe the sensation of an invisible force acting as your personal umbrella.

"You think that's weird," I said, "Imagine a bullet coming at you and bouncing off right in front of your face. That's a little too close for comfort."

"That is just about the coolest thing I've ever seen," Rusty remarked.

We continued on, and before too long, we made it to the iron rings. Dad finally took charge.

"Okay, Joseph, you go first with my wife. Hang on tight to each other and don't let go until we're all together again. Get out of the rings on the other side as soon as you get there, but stay together—don't let go for an instant. The boys and I will squeeze in and go next. Let's hope there's not something awful waiting there for us."

"Maybe I should just go real quick and come back—make sure that nothing's there," said Joseph.

My dad thought for a second, then agreed. I think he was scared that Joseph wouldn't return, and then we'd really not know what to do. Maybe it was better to stay together no matter what, and deal with what we had to deal with. But he reluctantly told Joseph to go ahead, but to come back immediately.

Joseph climbed into the rings, and soon vanished in a pillar of brief light.

We waited. Seconds dragged on and on. It was like trying

JAMES DASHNER ✧ 157

to fall asleep on Christmas Eve—every second lasted an hour. We waited and waited. And waited.

It was probably three minutes. It felt like three hours.

Joseph reappeared.

"Sorry, I tried just standing there, but nothing happened. You actually have to get out of the rings and climb back in for anything to happen. That's why it took longer than I thought it would. But here I am, and it looks safe. Come on, Helen, let's go."

Joseph hopped out, and my mom climbed into the rings with my dad's help. Then Joseph climbed back in. Soon came the same flash of light, and they were gone.

Dad didn't hesitate a second.

"C'mon guys, hurry up."

He basically lifted each of us in to the rings, then jumped in himself. We waited a few seconds, then felt the same light form around us in an instant, and then go away just as quickly as it had come.

We were in the Blackness again, right where Joseph and I had last left it.

It was damp and chilly, but it felt like a Georgia summer compared to the unbearable cold of that snowy world we had just left. I wondered if I would ever see that place again, or know what or where it was. It sure didn't seem like another planet or anything, but who knew.

We gathered around Joseph, and tried to decide what to do. We knew that there was no gate back to our world, and we also realized that none of us had the ability to rip the Black Curtain to get back there either.

We were discussing all of this, ready to start walking and see what happens, when things changed in a hurry, and our upside down world turned inside out.

A flash of light burst into view above us, and a horrible ripping sound blasted our ears right along with it. After the dismal light of the Blackness, the brilliant light coming down from above us blinded our eyes for a few seconds.

Feeling blind and scared, with our ears hurting from the horrible sound, we all fell down onto the circle of stone. I squinted up toward the light, and it looked like . . .

It looked like the opposite of the black holes we saw from our world when we were looking into the Blackness. We were looking into earthly daylight—the Black Curtain had been torn right before our eyes.

Several figures jumped through the rip, like parachuters going for a joyride, and landed with a thud just a few feet away from us. It reminded me of a gang of thugs jumping over a city fence into an alley, ready for a fight.

Standing before us, with the same wicked smiles we'd grown to know and hate, were Raspy Custer Bleak, Monster, Mayor Borbus T. Duck Jr., and Dontae the hairy gorilla.

✧CHAPTER 34✧

The Blocking of the Curtain

Raspy was dressed in a dark double-breasted suit, like he had come to a funeral or something. I had the strange thought that maybe it was our funeral, and that the ceremony wasn't going to be a very nice one.

Raspy lifted up his hand, and the hole to our world closed up and shot toward his hand, back into the shape of the same ball that he had used earlier in my house. But here in the Blackness, the ball was white instead of black. Strange. That ball was obviously some gift given to him by the Shadow Ka, to help him enter the Blackness whenever he wanted to. Then I remembered that Raspy *was* a Shadow Ka—his body was just being used. So it wasn't a gift, it was something the dang thing brought along for the trip.

Raspy's hand flashed under his suit coat and the white ball disappeared into a pocket somewhere.

"So, just as we'd planned. All together at once for the first time in a great while. It's so good to see you. All of you."

He paused, and walked over closer to me. He bent over, bore his beady, evil eyes into mine, and with his scratchy voice said, "Jimmy, I promise you will never escape me again. Now that we have you here, in the Blackness, with no way for you to get back to your pathetic little world, you have become what you disgusting people call a 'moot point.' I will admit, if for nothing else than to make you feel a little better before your life winks out like a wind-blown candle, that you had me a little scared for a while.

"So you made it to the First Gift. And a powerful Gift it is, Jimmy. I tried to find it, to put a stop to that miserable plan of the Givers which was doomed to fail from the beginning. I wanted to end it before it even began, but alas, you made it. But now you are here. You actually went after your family, you actually put three insignificant lives above an entire world. You are one selfish boy, Jimmy. And because of you, an entire world is going to die."

Raspy laughed, and walked back over toward his ugly men, and then spun around and looked back at me again.

"Once a person has received the First Gift, they are then the only—do you understand me—the only person that can receive the other Three. And the First is merely a help to obtain the others. Therefore, you are here, and the Gifts are there, and thus you have failed. The Ka will continue their preparations, no longer having to worry about the small chance that someone may obtain the Four Gifts, and they can proceed to lay the path for the future rulers of your world."

Raspy paused again, and gave me his patented evil grin.

"Tell me, do you really know what a Stomper is?"

"No," I said, putting all the hatred I could into the word.

"Have you ever had a nightmare, Jimmy? Have you ever been so terrified that you shook and got cold hands and had shivers go up and down your spine? Have you ever slept, ate, and drank fear?

"Well, imagine all the horrible things you possibly can— imagine them, Jimmy.

"That horror *is* the Stompers. And it won't be long before they will be ready to walk the path prepared for them by the Ka."

The mixture of Raspy's voice and the content of his words chilled me to the very center of my little body, and I was scared spitless. For the first time in a long time, I felt hopeless. I believed him. I believed it was all over.

But there was no way I would have ever done anything differently. Never, not in a million years, could I have left my family to die while I went off in search for things that I did not totally believe in yet. I had done the only thing I could have done, and if that meant the world I grew up in was lost, then I couldn't do a thing about it.

Shut up, I told myself. *A few words from the meanest, ugliest guy you've ever known and you're just going to give up? No*, I told myself. *No.*

There had to be a way.

My thoughts were cut off by a loud, piercing scream of fury. I looked around, expecting the Ka, when I realized that the horrible sound was coming from Raspy's mouth.

It stopped as abruptly as it had started. Raspy looked over at me and for a change, he didn't give me his famous smile. In fact, he looked worried, or anxious.

"Jimmy," he said, "I have given the call. It is time for you to die."

He pulled out his white ball and threw it up into the air, just to the side of him. The Black Curtain ripped, and once again I was looking through a window back into my world.

"Goodbye, Jimmy."

He started to jump for the rip in the Curtain, diving headfirst like an Olympic diver, and I suddenly knew that if he went through, we would all certainly die and it would all be over for us and for our little place we like to call Earth.

I sprung forward, diving for his feet as the tips of his hands started to enter the rip in the Curtain, as he started to leave the Blackness. I grabbed his left foot, holding on as hard as I had ever held onto anything in my life. His morons moved forward to stop me, but I called on the Shield without thinking, and their measly, evil hands could not touch me.

Not having learned a lesson from our previous encounter, they jumped back in surprise and alarm when they suddenly rebounded off of an invisible wall.

With my momentum combining with Raspy's, we both moved forward through the rip, toward home. He completely went through, and my hands also went through, clasped to his left foot, my hands went with him.

My dad sprang forward before Monster and the others could do anything, grabbed my legs, and yanked back towards himself as hard as he could. Both Raspy and I fell back out of the ripped Curtain and onto the stone circle, stumbling on top of each other.

While we shuffled to get up, Monster grabbed my mom by the neck and threw her around and into a headlock. Mayor Duck did the same to Rusty. Hairy calmly pointed a gun towards Joseph and my dad. It all happened at the same time, and before I could even stand up straight, we were back in a hopeless bind, despite my good-for-nothing efforts.

Raspy was furious.

"You little runt! You ignorant little southern trash!"

Raspy reached back and tried to slap me across the face. These bozos would never learn.

His hand bounced back violently, and he almost fell down. While he was off-balance, I kicked him in the side and he tumbled onto the stone circle hard.

"Stop it!"

It was Mayor Duck.

"Stop it, or you'll watch your whole family go to never-never land."

I looked around at him, and I had no idea what I could do to get out of this situation without taking a chance that my family would get hurt. I knew I was safe, but I also knew they weren't. My mind did roller coasters trying to think, but it was stuck in one of those loopty-loops.

I noticed a black cloud approaching from behind Mayor Duck and the rest of my family, heading towards us faster than any cloud could move. It was huge, and took up the whole sky. I knew what it was, and that there were a lot of them. They were back.

I yelled out to look in that direction, and then realized I was seemingly trying the oldest trick in the book. And they weren't going to fall for it. But Raspy saw it.

"My brothers are coming!" he yelled, like an insane man giddy with excitement, "They are coming for all of you!"

He jumped up and once again went for the rip in the Black Curtain.

I lunged for him again, but was too late. He vanished, and my arm went through the Curtain. And then everything happened at once.

The rip closed around my arm in an instant, leaving me not even the second I would need to take it out. It happened so fast that you couldn't even see it—one second there was a huge hole leading to brightness, the next it was gone.

Almost gone.

I guess if I had been a normal person, it would have cut my poor skinny arm right off, but I was not a normal person. I had The Shield, and the reaction of the tear in the Black Curtain to The Shield when it closed around it was as violent as intense thunder.

It seemed to explode the air around us, and hurled me twenty feet away from where I had been standing, so that I almost went into the surrounding waters. Everyone else fell to the ground hard, and everything around us began to shake like we were surrounded by a bunch of tap dancing T-rexes. We couldn't see any fire or explosions or anything, but we could feel violent disturbances in the air in every direction.

The Blackness had turned from a very scary place into the worst nightmare we'd ever had. It was like we were in an invisible war zone, and it worsened by the moment.

We all tried to stand, we tried to move around, we tried to crawl to each other. Monster and the others were no longer enemies—they only shared our sudden terror of exploding air and ear-piercing noises and shaking. The Black Curtain was ripping and closing and ripping and closing in places here and there all over the place. The stone circle began to crack and one side of it suddenly shot up in the air like a submarine had just surfaced below it. The inky, silvery waters began to bubble and spit out huge geysers of liquid in every direction. The path was warping and buckling.

We didn't know what, but something very awful was happening.

I caught a glance in the direction of the black cloud. It wasn't a cloud anymore.

Hundreds, if not thousands of flying Shadow Ka were once again heading straight for us, and they weren't taking their time about it. They would be on us in minutes.

I crawled desperately toward my mom. Dad and Joseph did the same. Rusty was with Mom. Monster, Duck, and Hairy made their way toward the iron gates, trying to escape into the frozen world. I didn't give a hoot about them.

The circle was breaking up all around me, shooting up huge chunks into the air, and they came crashing down all around us. I knew if I didn't get to my family quick, they'd be hurt something awful, if not killed.

I finally put my feet up under me, and heaved myself forward, and fell right beside my mom. Rusty was clinging to her with every ounce of strength he had. Dad lurched this way and that, and finally stumbled on top of me. Joseph soon followed.

The air continued to explode all around us, and the

roar was deafening. We could barely make out the terrible screams of the Shadow Ka as they got closer and closer.

I grabbed my dad around the neck, pulled him close, and threw the both of us on top of my mom and Rusty.

"Everybody hold onto me!" I yelled with every bit of vocal chord I could muster. "Hold onto me!"

We threw our arms around each other this way and that, until we had become the closest-knit family hug in history. Joseph managed to crawl over to us as well, and joined the hug. We clung together, making sure that everyone was touching me, knowing that the only thing we had now was each other. And the Shield.

A hurricane of wind hit us, and then came the storm of Shadow Ka.

Screaming their bloody murder, sounding like a million screeching dinosaurs, they flew at us.

A new noise joined the melee—the sound of hundreds of desperate, flying Shadow Ka bouncing off an invisible Shield. It sounded like a spray of countless pellets hitting a wall of bullet-proof glass. We could see shadows and terrible glimpses of claws and faces and teeth and arms and legs and wings all around us, dropping and bouncing and screaming and gnashing. We were truly in a nightmare.

The Shield held.

They did not stop. They kept coming and coming. I thought how stupid they must be to not give up. Or maybe they thought they could break the Shield. *Maybe they could*, I suddenly thought. Maybe we ought to get the heck out of here.

"Let's try to stand up!" I screamed.

The ground still shook, the Ka still bombarded us, the air continued to explode and the Black Curtain continued to rip open and close all around us. But there was just no way to make it to those openings in the short time they appeared.

They came and went too fast.

Our only choice was the frozen world.

We gathered ourselves, still clinging to each other desperately, and somehow orchestrated what must've been the funkiest looking move ever. As a fivesome, we all stood up. We clung to each other in a circle of hugs now.

"Let's sidestep our way to the iron rings!" Dad yelled.

The wind from a thousand beating wings of Shadow Ka roared around us as we clumsily made our way to the iron gateway. Several times we fell down from the shaking, almost breaking the life-grip we had on each other. Somehow, we held on. The Shield stayed true.

We were getting closer and closer, the Shadow Ka were not letting up, the air did not calm down. Every effort we could summon from every inch of our body and souls, we threw into the task of making it to those iron rings.

We got to within ten feet.

That was the closest we would ever get.

✧ ✧ ✧

Suddenly, in the middle of all that wind and sound and terror, the girl—the Giver—appeared right in front of us—one second she was not there, the next second she was. She was not dressed as I had seen her in the cave under the Door. She wore a flowing blue dress, which almost looked metallic and sparkled with every move she made. Her hair was also different, put up in some fancy hair-do like she was going to the prom. But her expression had not changed. She still looked like the saddest girl that had ever taken a breath.

Unlike the first time I had met her, I now knew what she was. Or at least, I knew what she was called. I still didn't know much about what it meant.

A Giver.

She stepped forward and leaned towards my ear.

Somehow the words she spoke were easy to hear and understand despite the deafening roar of the Ka and quaking stone. It was especially strange since it was obvious that she was whispering.

"You have caused a great violence in the Blackness. The First Gift has not failed us. You have blocked the Black Curtain, shielded your world from ours. This Ripping may be the last for some time, so quickly, now, I cannot hold it for long."

With her words, a tear in the Black Curtain opened right behind her. A burst of earthly sunlight shone through, making me squint hard, like I used to when Mom would wake me up for school by turning on the light. Unlike the constant ripping and closing that was going on all around us, this one stayed open. But it seemed to be wavering a little, like it wasn't stable. We didn't wait to gander at it too long.

With a combined effort, and with no need for me to relay the girl's words to the rest of my family, we surged forward in one combined push toward the opening.

And then, despite all that I had been through, the most terrible thing I've ever witnessed occurred.

As we made for the familiar air of our home world, Joseph slipped and fell to the trembling stone below us. He lost his grip on my arm and waist, and before we could even register in our little brains what was happening, he was gone.

A pack of Shadow Ka grabbed him in a million places, lifted him into the air, and flew away, disappearing behind another black horde of Ka. His screams were drowned out in an instant, replaced by the same awful sounds that had been with us for what seemed like an eternity.

I had never known such pure distress and pain. Joseph was gone. We all stared in shock and horror, as my mom's screams pierced the air as she instinctively tried to follow the direction in which he'd disappeared. Dad and I held onto her, firmly keeping her from running into the same fate as Joseph. Our hearts were aching, our minds were racing with panic and fear, our blood boiled with rage for what had just happened.

He was gone. Gone. Taken by creatures that were nothing but evil.

The girl spoke again, and this time she did not whisper.

"There is nothing you can do! You must go, now! NOW!"

All of us knew that she was absolutely right. It was terrible, horrible, unspeakable, but she was right. We could do nothing for Joseph. We were in a hurricane of shadow and earthquake and terrible noise. The world around us was collapsing.

Acting on impulse, feeling like we had abandoned him without even trying, we did as she said.

We went through.

As the furious sound of insane shadow wings faded into the sudden quiet of a summer afternoon in Georgia, I heard the girl say some last words.

"You have blocked the Black Curtain. Use your time wisely."

And then, just as the hole into the Blackness sealed shut, I barely made out her final sentence, and it would baffle me and my family for a long time to come.

"Do not worry, I will die for your friend."

✧Epilogue✧

Somehow we knew that Joseph was okay. We had survived pure terror, and he was probably still in the middle of it, but somehow we knew he was okay. The Givers would save him, and one day we would see him again. We just knew it. Well, at least, we sure hoped it.

And for the first time in days, I felt like maybe I could relax—just a little bit. It was completely dark outside the huge Japan Airlines plane, and the loud but relaxing hum of the jet engines had lulled the rest of my family into a deep sleep. They all looked like they'd never had a care in the world. I knew better. None of us could get over the pain of losing Joseph, despite the hope given to us by the girl's last words. I was just glad they could finally sleep. Who knew what danger lay ahead in Japan.

Japan.

I was going to Japan. What would I have said two weeks ago if somebody had told me that I'd be flying to Japan soon? Of course, that would have been the least strange of the things somebody could have told me about my future two weeks ago. Going to Japan? Strange, but okay, maybe. Going to Japan to find a book to tell me how to save the world? That would have been a hard story to bite and chew.

It had been the only thing we could do. We knew the book was in Japan, and we knew that the book was our only hope right now. We had no idea how long the Black Curtain would be blocked, and we had no idea what we would do when and if it opened again. But the book could maybe help us find the other Gifts, and hopefully those would lead us to figuring out how to get Joseph back and how to save the world from the enemy that we had never even seen.

When we had gone through the rip in the Black Curtain, out of that horror caused by the Curtain closing around the Shield, there had been no sign of Raspy. And that, of course, would remain a concern. But we still had seen no sign of him, and had come to realize that there were things far scarier than Raspy. We hoped against hope that maybe the blocking of the Curtain had somehow ripped the Shadow Ka from his mind or something.

Anyway, I thought, for now, it was time to relax. Strange how life goes on despite the bizarre turns that our lives take. After everything we'd seen and done, I was still a kid who was tired and uncomfortable as heck in a tiny plane seat. I leaned back in my seat—the whole two inches—and closed my eyes.

Instead of sleep, a million thoughts poured into my noggin.

I couldn't help but think about all that I had been through. It was all just too crazy, too unreal to believe. But I didn't doubt for a second that it was all true. I'd finally come to accept it all—every bit of it. Life wasn't what I and all my family and friends had imagined it to be.

It was a lot more strange.

And a lot more terrifying.

But that's the way it was, and that's the way it was going to be. I just had to accept it, and move on and see what I could do about it in this new life I had discovered.

My thoughts then drifted to all the things I had been through.

The tree, and Mayor Duck, and seeing that woman disappear. The mansion where I first met Raspy and Monster.

Salt Lake City and Joseph. Hairy and the boat. Old Willow. The Door. The Shield. The Blackness.

Shadow Ka, and Joseph come back from the dead.

My little family's escape from death and the blocking of the Black Curtain. Joseph, gone, in a cloud of dark monsters.

No doubt about it—this boy had just been through one heck of an adventure. I wished it were all just a book and I could close it and be done. No chance of that, I reckoned.

I settled in, tipped my Braves hat down over my eyes— Dad had bought me a new one at the airport store, like the awesome dad he is—and it wasn't too long before the waves of sleep started to wash away the sands of my endless thoughts and nightmares.

I really did feel like things were safe for now, that all we had to do was go to Japan and figure things out. The Black Curtain was blocked, after all. And deep down, I just knew that somehow Joseph was safe, or at least alive. Surely, things were looking on the upside for us.

And after everything we had been through, one thing stood above all others. The love I had for my family was endless, and the power of it would pull us through to the bitter end, whatever that end may be.

So, flying at thirty thousand feet in a Japan Airlines airliner, heading for the exotic lands of Japan, I, Jimmy Fincher, holder of the First Gift, defeater of Shadow Ka, blocker of the Black Curtain, the most powerful person in the world, closed my eyes, and drifted off to dreamland.

It was downright boring compared to my real life.

ABOUT THE AUTHOR

James Dashner was born and raised in Georgia but now lives in Utah with his wife and three children. He is currently working on a new series. James loves to hear from his readers. You can email him at author@jamesdashner.com. Please visit his website as well: www.jamesdashner.com.

ABOUT THE ILLUSTRATOR

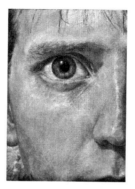

Michael Phipps grew up spending hours with friends drawing, imagining other worlds, making odd recordings, and building marble chutes and forts. He always knew he would be an artist as an adult, and he graduated with a bachelor of fine arts degree in illustration from the University of Utah. He loves to spend time with his family and friends, be outdoors, and listen to strange music. His art can be viewed at www.michaelphipps.net. E-mail him at art@michaelphipps.net.